the blue rental

Also by Barbara Mor:

*The Great Cosmic Mother: Rediscovery
of the Religion of the Earth* (1987)

Barbara Mor is native to southwest American coast & desert (SoCal,
NM, AZ). Beyond invisible authorship of The First God [The Great
Cosmic Mother], her work has appeared in OrpheusGrid, Sulfur,
BullHead, Mesechabe, Ms., Trivia (US); Ecorche, Intimacy,
Spectacular Diseases (UK); all print journals & mostly defunct.
Online recent work occurs on TriviaVoices.net, (Feb 05-Sept 08);
CTheory.net (Aug 4, 2005-Sept 30, 2010); & Woodslot.com, (April 4,
2008-Oct 21, 2010); cool Canadian editors! Adam Engel's interview
with Barbara Mor, *24/7 & Yr Dreams*, appeared on DissidentVoice.org,
June 14, 2004, & Mor's Preface to Engel's Topiary, *Mything Persons*,
is on DissidentVoice.org, Oct 13, 2008.

the blue rental

by

Barbara Mor

The Oliver Arts & Open Press
2578 Broadway, Suite #102
New York, NY 10025
http://www.oliveropenpress.com

ISBN: 978-0-9819891-6-7

Library of Congress Control Number: 2011922551

These pieces have appeared in the following online & print sites & are printed here with the kind
permission of their editors, specifically, in the case of CTheory, www.ctheory.net, the editors
Arthur and Marilouise Kroker.

> 'oasis.' *CTheory: 1000 Days of Theory*, editors Arthur & Marilouise
> Kroker, University of Victoria, BC, www.ctheory.net, August 4, 2005

> 'HERE: a small history of a mining town in the American southwest,
> 1985.' *1000 Days of Theory*, December 15, 2005

> 'sea of hunger.' *CTheory: 1000 Days of Theory*, April 12, 2006

> 'oasis2.' *CTheory: 1000 Days of Theory*, April 3, 2008;
> www.woodslot.com, editor Mark Woods, April 4, 2008; with links to 'oasis,' 'HERE,'
> and 'sea of hunger'

> 'the missing girls.' *CTheory: 1000 Days of Theory*, December 3,
> 2008; woodslot, December 6, 2008

> 'oasis3.' *CTheory: Resetting Theory*, October 20, 2009; woodslot,
> November 13, 2009

> 'the blue rental.' *CTheory: Theory Beyond the Codes*, September 30,
> 2010; woodslot, October 21, 2010

The following 2 pieces have appeared in Trivia, www.triviavoices.net & in Sulfur (print) and are
included here with the permission of the editors:

> 'hypatia.' Trivia: Voices of Feminism 7-8, www.triviavoices.net, editors Lise Weil and
> Harriet Ellenberger, September, 2008

> 'Linguistic Duplex.' *Sulfur* 35, editor Clayton Eshleman, Eastern Michigan University,
> Ypsilanti, MI, Winter, 1994

Excerpts from HERE appear in *Against Civilization: Readings and Reflections*, editor John
Zerzan, Uncivilized Books, 1999; Enlarged Edition, Feral House, 2005

to Clayton Eshleman
from a Tucson BurgerKing
con respeto

CONTENTS

the blue rental   1

rapture   13

sea of hunger   23

oasis   31

HERE: a small history of a mining town in the
American southwest, 1985   43

Linguistic Duplex   67

oasis2   93

hypatia   103

the missing girls   133

oasis3   147

the blue rental

the blue door and blue windows radiate the mind of the house
like a small timid brain sitting in a dark room radiates its
obsession with a terrible distance
or (sunk in earth a thin fish learns to walk the ocean floor
climbs blue walls and angular canyons restless up into us the
same spine you think) the emptiness of the house once a
thought as desert once a sea house a planet neighborhood of
suburban stars occupy the same distance
    it is a desert abode with cactus in the yard bugs or a lizard
    seeking moisture no shade yet it is all watery and blue the
    psychic color a wavelength all creatures see in our original
    dream this radiation
the original dream a television in the corner of a deep room
always on like insomnia the ancestors squat half submerged
in this uterine earth pictures go in and out of human eyes and
they cannot sleep
they cannot sleep   along the night street as along the hull of
a sunken ship portholes glow with bloated faces or a submarine
occupied by phosphorescence radiates a blue music from its

inward silence (it smokes a blue cigarette with long blue lips)
as time has sunk here wedged between backyards and tall
antennae of loneliness with many eyes and ears wired to a
skulls curved dish sad rooftops waiting lonely dials turned
endlessly   the static of blue light emits this silence and
they do not sleep as the sea recedes
 in the desert a dark luminous thing a foliage and dust
 of awful presence it remembers the sea it began in a black
 ocean with thoughts before stars entered an eye or a
 small door   and i do not remember the crime it saw
a crime always occurring in blue insomnia like the sea

1.
it was alone
it was a mushroom (perhaps) a blue nagual who always lived
here its little adobe on the desert surrounded by more desert
etc etc and nothing
it was an experiment
it was not an experiment but a need or a poem or a fatality
(from the inventor of fate a joke)
the invention of fiction of friction of evil (resultant)
altho so beautiful and night illuminant with stars
i did not invent
i did not invent
it was alone with some idea
i think of primeval things   veins of moth wings spinal
auras long magnetic shudders a blue volcanic breathing and
eruptions of thick earth as fire continents swell and recede
shift under them episodes pulse into them on blue wires
strange night animals traverse a blue horizon as herds and
constellations of some imagination become their skins and
eyes reflect and copy this enormous theater   huge centuries
of mind and hunger begun with pale telluric flickers
i do not remember trajectories of humans or their dream
except the eyes empty screen when their story ends a brain
reads remote transmission of grave shapes emptying slowly
of blood while blue light pours in or one world swallows
another or great histories implode the disembodied voices
of absolute blue space and a blue radiation of the dead who
are still awake
 a mural of genitals blue orgasms of horses a

the blue rental

blue photograph of night with many spines exposed houses
where the crime occurred corpses emitting spliced cries a wall
of switches lamps mirrors and other sad fixtures of eyes
      how blue thought meets dark night as a screen of dots
      bizarrely weeping or gesturing spasmodically to the eyes
      center which is death   of walls exploded as flowers
bullets of fish swimming beautiful creatures dancing among
veins of blue fluorescence ganglia of mind transformed
from sleep into an empty room (this is when the crime who
dwells no one lives now sits in a dark room only)

to live vicariously(a mud body)and then forget   *i dwelt*
among circulating particles polyps coral rays amorphous living
jellies (inhale and exhale a blue smoke as if breathing time
before it begins) ominous reptiles insects persons thickly
swum or crushed into air like fetal planets   a list of
existences i forget
                        how blue light pours from eyes
ears mouths as a terrible stream of distances a blue absence
hemorrhaging as far as galaxies   *the crime inhabits*
it gazes alone into this hallucinated blue thing   it is

2.
there was a sidewalk alley asphalt *cement and minerals* a
yard of dust and rusted metal where the stars become hard
perhaps someone slept on a bare bedspring or hung clothes
on a single line or in and out of my little clay house with
a clay pot holding dry earth and no flowers
      a world (being) of dying animals thirst or species
of local thought   rented cheap as a root sucks up moisture
enough for one day it could be a hotel a corpse or a planet
transient in time a blue water occurred and then siphoned
by a sun (as i imagine) the memory of squid and salt moon
residue of scorpion and rock circling my neighborhood the
horses were here great nebula and premonitions of heroic
drama their black manes on fire   and cities are
beyond in some chemistry of the mind but not yet
o yes   Orion
chronically to look up gaze upward into codes 1.5million
years their time humans and Orion who was the first hunter
he strides forward eastward westward one blue foot one red

shoulder exploding a club raised or an arrow shot to theBull
who does not seem to die   or stands brightly his belt 3
absolute stars and a sword a dagger a penis hung down M42
a nebulous groin from which other suns erupt and spin out
this giant gaseous cloud(or Firedrill orFriggerock Osiris one
hemisphere or another)   the most distant constellation it
remains constant longest unchanged as they evolve under it
name it shift and shape themselves as if inhabitants also of
this zodiac   the blue Picts ran around with starry animals
tattooed on their bodies theMayan Hearth 3 stones DayZero
13.0.0.0.0 the gods descend to set it up a mirror of Orion
or that is what they saw or said they saw imprinted on the
night   before all other transmissions the first transmission
burned into night they branded cattle and their own flesh
or written on a poetry high calligraphy of their blood as
eloquence of some kind *seared on a brain* who was the
original predator or dreamer gazing so far   their eye or the
stellar pictures real meat or patterns of white dots
                some say a hunter a man with his dogs a dark
horse(andSirius andMonoceros) but i recall deserts or ash or
hot vents of the sea also blind grope on the sea floor open
and close mouth gullet breathing water food or otherwise
existent as mud i am clay under stars (clay as flesh as *lodo
barro* distinct from *spirit* they say but nothing exists but this
Mind euphoriant) i see code a message a language *zodiakos
kyklos* killed by a Scorpion they say   i am required to look
upward translate the black sky flickery images where the
story begins
                recalling sea floor Trilobite and worm 520 million bce
Cambrian explosion scavenger tracks consumes a blind worm
the brain grows by seeing seizing consuming armored as a tank
a shaggy thing liceshape with fly eyes it has eyes crawls swims
moves like a machine 1/8 inch to over 2 feet (28") grows by
watching into watching sees the jelly the starfish the sponge a
blind worm as it will conquer sea land air imagination over
all Trilobitomorpha first predator first thing with eyes and the
eyeless prey they gaze at each other worm and hunter one
thing with eyes one thing desired
                                i did not invent
the distance between this long immersion   and the stars

3.

when they brought the horses i knew them   a crack in the
universe a fissure in mind look up the Milky Way divides the
sky into 2 hemispheres a brain 100,000,000,000 stars in
this brain a mythos in the sky with a brain as mirrors slow
transit of codes in the particulars of their eyes they will say
they are not entertained by such discourse a memory where
they do not live or think they live but the horse burst from rock
crevice in a sidewalk all from Time returned little *eohippus*
dawn horse Dawn of mammals 53 million years Eocene in the
West as their hands on cave walls opened mineral flesh and
it was there(30,000bce Aurignacian)evolutions later and
all the beasts emergent from a stony hole or cavernous mind
dark and shining like night

                            no doubt they told stories the
passage of time 40,000 years 3 million years a long time as
busy with rock fire water umbilical ropes they climb in and
out of bodies make animal noises   what goes in and out of
bodies a fascination of their minds they look for something
hidden sex eclipse death scenarios ofTime a great book or
mystery the stars are writing or inside skulls ominous viscera
and arts of bone hunters gleaners watchers song and dance
as the animals move over and over their eyes they tell retell
this story as if a script or a dream   in this dream they carry
spears knives needles calendars a wheel a toy transistor
radios and laundromat hands engines in their tongues and 10
fingers how to count how seeds grow powers of wounds and
replications fire speech and murder as original inventions

   they begin to believe they are not animals but masters of
something the zoo and the mirror appear together 4500bce
for who they are faces beautiful things collected in search
of what is hidden soft clay like another flesh impressed again
and again with hard numbers how to rule how to plunder how
to conquer who they are animals upright and glorious on
horse machines when they wrote as hands fisted with Signs
granaries measures maps ofThought very agile with chariots
pyramids empires suddenly very smart hands on legal pages
scripting History(asImmortality) as the universe moves over
and over their eyes blur and forget the human gaze derives
from pain night eating death and killing what is beautiful
this is not hidden

the horses belong here rampant extinct
12,000 years hunted down by ancestors eaten returned 1493
their drivers as giant Trilobites out of the sea out of air who
cannot believe they are glorious *piles of corpses raised* and
streaming blood up to their knees this machinery moves
like the sky relentless and sexual over earthly bodies their
favorite story when they were not weeping or mopping up or
reproducing it as spectacle as automatons flash their metals and
electric eyes indeed i watch it as they watched themselves
for they suffered inside what is hidden going in and out of
their animal Time asMinds and stars move over and over their
repeated patterns the thing hidden they have not found
and clearly i do not care

4.
extremophiles in deep vents of the sea sulfuric and blind
do they suffer   the weight of oceans and total dark 248F
they boil but do not boil shrimp bacteria tubeworms 10'
long chemistry eats them and vice versa or cannibalize each
other they survive *do we suffer*   volcanic BlackSmokers
colonies in frail papery tubes Pompeii worm 5' long pale
gray red gills on heads like feathers most extreme gradient
temperatures protrude from tubes heads cool 79F at other
end their tails at 176F centuries and centuries as Vesuvius
erupts 79ce a Roman city also Pompeii did not survive
or ice 12' deep solid –4F Atacama desert of ice little bits of
dirt embedded provide chemical nutrients as permafrost
or goldmines Africa 6 miles deep microbes eat cracks eat
rock or fungi algae acidbathed eat red water thickly iron like
blood   tubeworms 8' long 250 years old or 4-5 centuries
old Gulf of Mexico older than conquistadores eating oil
no oxygen no dreams what do they know
          Piezophiles PsychroCryophiles Lithoautotrophs
Metalotolerants a black well cesspool pozo negro pitch lake
liquid asphalt (La Brea 38,000 years oldest material wood
or bone) wolves bison horse groundsloth turtles snails fish
millipede lion tiger mammoth dead bones the animals
struggled here no way out no air microbes bacteria
archaë   the ancestors live here

          it was a story existence 4.54 billion years
microscopic particles ofNothing become something on their

dark sides required to make Worlds methane ammonia
hydrogen + electric spark and watched itself walk into such
proliferation *the phenomenon called life* it multiplied
itself carbonic acids water nitrogenous compounds it
could be Extreme to manifest imagination from Itself as
slimemold moves over and over dung or rot to make a film
grotesque minuscules selfreplicate as if 2 lovers out ofOne
as plants or Echiniscus may reproduce themselves lizards
Daphnia fungus worm our ancestors the precursors in their
dying varieties
        and what evolved into them not a crime but
fascination with their crime

       Homo faber hands on cave walls red black ocher
charcoal fixed with animal fat where water trickles from
rock a painted wound earth makes beautiful things (no
the first mirror before Egypt Ur a still pool the gaze of water
where they met the Other the shiningHunter the first zoo
was here dark gallery of primal beasts desired by the eye
they too looked back at other beasts blind luminal beasts
mining ore from their flanks and udders *we watch we want*
what they killed they loved with attention   iron manganese
lightning ash the chemistry of thought and their metalurged
hands amazing hands brains as pistons grinding everything
down into final dust as if heroic waste lavish waste as if
endlessly prolific as the starry letters or genetic code
       hold up a mirror to Nature they said and
can be extreme a luxury of pain   their incriminant bodies
shoved down on spikes or pikes pushed up anus thru mouth
or burn alive or crush with religious stones ancestors die
with teeth clenched on grass their green mouths try to eat
grass like cattle or some breathe terminal gas or choked
in soil mephitic environs of their history or biscuits of lard
salt and dirt they eat dirt as nutrient as do all things   and
walk into themselves a blue screen generations of mirrors
a story as dark sides shadows emerge from light excreting
darkness even death erotic
       a poetry of sweat of their bodies and perfume and
on the screen it shines luxuriously Alkaliphiles Mypoliths
Radioresistants Zerophiles Polyextremophiles
do they suffer   or kill in some trance of surrender

or what says too much pain (they said) it must
stop now   (an intention not a result)

their cold eyes derive from eating ice lust fear and loving
Night who fills up emptiness with constellations their crime
derives from Time orNight who fills up thought with signs
it was a story up there Orion his horse and dogs the Hunter
who walks out of black light into intelligent eyes his black
mind shines luxuriously inside a constant skull   they
walk in anywhere and switch on the light begin to Think
watch read gaze want something beyond the wall hidden in
a wall turn off the light and stare at the wall until they can
walk thru it *what exists* the other side *inextremis*Mind
it is a talent gift a compulsion why do we love as
bleeding animals they have erased us
Bison Mammoth Aurochs GreatAuk Ursus spelaeus

Mousterian Magdalenian pressured into stone human hands
marks runes hieroglyphs phonemes alphabets codex of fire
if in Ebla they wrote it down if Tulum Punt Aptera they
construct it   utopia Atlantis NewWorld 'symbolic mastery'
which is a cosmic impulse or irony   culminating Life
who loved everything they killed truly for the huge beauty
of it power of forms exploding rock wall thought in and out
of eyes lucid and gone the fixity ofMind who can inhabit
all this yet still Hidden   *it was a story*
new Atlantis(to end suffering) in eyes a mirror cosmic dust
and screen on which to watch it   Epic suffering
NewAtlantis MAGNALIA NATURAE(Natural Magic1627)
             the list begins with 'the prolongation of life'
             & ends with 'Artificial minerals and cement'
there is no pity required the great story(it is said) proceeds

water bears Tardigrades slow walkers some parthenogenic
alive in Himalayas deep seas polar caps equator on mosses
lichens liverworts temps close to absolute zero –460F hot as
303F survive 1000 X more radiation than other animals or
a decade 200 years without water 10 days in vacuum space
or subsurface ocean water Jupiters moon hydrothermal vents
on sea floor a distant Moon something will dwell and copy
this sidewalks made of seashells where egRomans invented

the blue rental

Concrete   sand clay paste of ancient calcium

the Horseshoe crab (cf Trilobite larval stage spiders scorpions
also related) over 300 million years Cambrian *xiphosurid*
onto a beach a sidereal sidewalk

nothing is so vast as things that are empty

5.
blue womb or rental room of empty houses inside a vast night
blue abodes along a street are radiant with such light strangely
occupied as museum or uterus blue immense of a universe
looped and rerun perpetual for the stars insomnia   who never
sleep   it cant get born out of in which it always dwells
                              or who lives in the other rooms
who knows why they continue to love it watching static when
the show is over or now stare at a blue screen   *a hypnotic*
stare injects blue into everything 1 light year is 6trillion miles
so they do not sleep or dream trance is a slower brain as
gods watch an indifferent spectacle
     Devonian 395-345million yearsbce swamps forests ferns
     something crawls from sea to wet green then fish may walk
     4limbed vertebral land dwellers 360millionyearsbce repeat
     250million dinosaurs 65million mammals 8million hominids
     humans 200,000 years   from explosions of Cambrian
     multicells Great Ordovician biodiversification   methane
     ammonia hydrogen+lightning spark=amino acids 3.5billion
     years   a universe they say 13.75 billion years   began
that eyes stare at such distance   or the crime it means
        what is a chronic absence to do with enormous pain
to create an Other to end the Solitude of Everything that IS
it *gropes* blind first invention of feelers eyes beauty words
i look up at starry mirrors and desire translation into words
and becomes what it has become   i am therefore i am
i am not obscure   *i do not remember the crime*

as pyramids record days years huge stone blocks of Time
fractures of earth below great cities or deserts once jungles
of submerged night
i am positioned here to read stars one lightyear 5.88 trillion
miles the closest star 8000 times more distant than farthest

planet whatever it may be relatively changeless constellations
but they do slowly drift   ram fish wolf unicorn whale
worm and crab the Vulva and some poets singing head a
black cavernous wound into residues of bodies of worlds
galaxies so condensed they are reborn into seeds eggs sperm
i watch them go over   mustang bull jaguar slow motion
over a horizon as over a cliff into some chasm but reappear
each night season year *zodiakos kyklos* once horizon of
heroes and beasts in amnesias of desert air the ancestors
watch them become extinct in solemn entertainment we
gaze into each disappearance   await our turn

most distant from earth(1500 lightyears)Orion thus remains
recognizable longest observable constellation parallel to the
rise of human species and civilizations so far and so slow to
change the Hunter but relentless as all things   Orion shifts
into a giant vague X   the ancestors watch it happen

to escape or reconsider a universe recedes horses vault or
gallop backwards into sidewalk fissures oceans of dust or ice
return to cities intricate architecture then melt disperse words
come from human mouths hang as frost voices in blue air
then they burst with invisible rays from their bold eyes
exploding a violent universe desires of fluorescence radiant
desires 8000 times as far as most distant planet florescent open
in the night but my eye is lonely for something else
                                        perhaps
i sing with long blue lips incantations of the next thing or
whisper what dinosaur blood human blood other lost excretions
transform into what chemical or mineral compression of
65 million years   in mirrors of permafrost sand or glass
the view of exotic lights cacti radiant with uranium mercury
flown thru war rubble and wriggling worms thru dirt   bluish
hallucinations of oceanic and extreme lifeforms urban future
submarine mansions or 100 foot tall fungi on stilts or stairways
climb from seafloor to a Moon everyone knows it can be done
dogs are born with many eyes(Kerberos) or no eyes the eyes
are elsewhere tomatoes swimming upstream and frogs with 13
eyes in their throats and their throats are seeing and eyes are
singing   and o it does not stop
some blueprint in the mud my mind such as it is recorded

the blue rental

amnesias of solitude(exaltation)among my planets biostructure
my little house in space the blue adobe of a flesh that is all
radiant and cold unsleeping furnace of stars a blue agitation
without memory but how to reset forget all this and begin
again
o how vast

***   ***   ***   ***

Materials quoted:

cement & minerals
>Francis Bacon, New Atlantis (1627) MagnaliaNaturae list, 488-9

piles of corpses i raised
>Royal Archives of Ebla (a repeated phrase)
>Ebla—an ancient city of SW Asia near the site of Aleppo, Syria. The
>cuneiform Ebla Tablets (discovered 1974-5) describe a thriving 3rd
>millennium bce civilization centered around the city. A Semitic
>language & people.

the phenomenon called life
>Aldous Huxley, Literature & Science (1963)

there is no pity required the great story
>"Let all pity be alien to those who watch
>a crime, not only by the hunter who cunningly fulfills
>what time allows.
>*Killing is a form of our wandering sorrow.*
>Whatever happens to us will in time
>be right, for spirit is serene, pure & still."
>>Rilke, Sonnets to Orpheus XI, trans. Willis
>>Barnstone (2004), 177

nothing so vast as things that are empty
>'But it is the empty things that are vast, things solid are most contracted.'
>Francis Bacon, last paragraph of Preface to The Great Instauration (1620)
"Nothing is so vast as things that are empty"
>Paul Virilio paraphrase, City of Panic, trans Julie Rose (2005), 133

a hypnotic stare injects blue into everything
>Malcolm de Chazal, Sens-Plastique (1947) 2008 trans. Irving Weiss; Barry
>Schwabsky review BookForum   Feb/March 2009, 28

it gropes blind feelers eyes words
>'Natural selection indeed *"gropes"* --blindly sends out feelers...' -- Richard
>Wright, Non-Zero (2000), 314

barbara mor

Rapture

this girl was born whose cunt was a heart. almost, like
Jesus. child of dust, begot spit out on a beige rug in a
trailerpark outside Zion(utah) some know from the beginning
without knowing(holiness). mother 3 brothers a big man who
fed and beat them all biblically called father except her.
at first the youngest called baby girl then my girl as she
grew into it, daughter of loins pentecosts of alcohol the alibis
longsuffering wind a desert cannot bloom except our tongues
are whips the wound enjoys its blood burst. this was her name
  she grew without anyone paying strict attention. legs
stretched out in the dirt with stones for pet animals. the
father itinerant worker drunk when nasty often unemployed pulled
her on his knees pawed her, reek of tobacco beer truckoil sweat
in his magnified face abrasions on her small neck thighs and
cheeks. age 5 the mother died suddenly of cerebral hemorrhage.
then school, 10 mile busride to and from outskirts cinderblock
classroom 3 angry brothers troubles precede her, she was not
like them. a soft child on asphalt playground, little boys
gave pennies dimes or candy to see and touch it, then she might

want to kiss and they ran away. a teachers notes piled up, father
workaccident disability, they move further south into another
state another truckstop trailerpark rock cactus garden chickenpen
and ax always leaned against the feathery wire. sick rage
unoccupied he became a preacher Bible-ranting at them mealtable
fried eggs chicken potatoes wonderbread beer milk bad leg and
back swelling belly gut over his cowboy levis belt soiled t-shirt
he banged his fists in their face like God, on the table into
the heat and frothing at the mouth of chickenblood fear of dead
gods flies always assaulting what lives like martyrdom, all the
Old Testament and gospel Revelations passages he spewed out
into their eyes ears stomachs were terrible without knowing
anything(churched) they knew that life so far was Evil. his
fingers smelled like fish often when they ate no fish. when he
moved to incest outright sleep with her every night he made her
first pray with him to this god forgiveness of a father, on
their knees together, then into the bed in the trailer alcove
where it could not be seen. they heard, and knew the paradigm
of Innocence was her flesh somehow her exclusion from his dumb
fists saved them, on her part, from Death by terror. thus was
the desert of agony without remission endured, as daily parable.
    not until she bled all over the couch, like some
chicken he beheaded in the yard, upon her first bleeding(menarche)
so much she stained the only chair in the room he sat in skyblue
imitation leather stuffed 'house of hell' he stripped his belt
from his own thick flesh and welted her bare thighs and exposed
buttocks before them for now and future sin was abruptly real
(she cast out Demons, or leprosy, or lust with no moral consequence
in exchange for being a Child but now she looked back as conscious
woman. his worked-up sweat dripped on her, tears also, she
forgave him 12 year old girl inflamed and bruised sitting on
Daddys lap petting his sobbing hair)
    each brother in that 114degree summer grew taller than him
and left, 123 together only short of murder. she began to cook, left
school became the one who cleaned and thought ahead, distribution
of the money as he further sank into sullen fat incoherence. age
15 she took a parttime waitress job truckstop café ½ mile up
their road this proved lethal peering into mirage of yard one
afternoon he saw the motorcycle pull up laughing she jumped off
30 year old male straddling semen reached for her arm leans too
close into her breasts, as she pulled free waved approached

trailersteps the motorcycle not reving off but watching her in
preparation of raising his swollen stiff fist to smack her he
suffered massive stroke stopped aghast by Vision of blood
everywhere before his eyes, he fell unconscious. she entered a
dead man.

the other waitress(fulltime,26) moved in with her car and
boyfriends, and the girl always seemed younger and older than her
age both wise and childlike, assuming virgin they came in late
whispering drunken in darkness foreplay and intercourse on the
livingroom beige rug while she in the alcove bed usually woke to
hear as if herself dreamed far away. they teased her and the boyfriends
were able to suggest evenings with her when the other worked late,
ease of deception among males rarely sober but consistent they came
and went a dozen varieties of basic trucker biker cowboy who lived
on a moving animal always moving on while the waitress and the
girl served food and comfort, on the job.

4-5 local boys her age smelled
heat on the wind always passing on her road, hung out at the café
dated movies at the outdoor screen where no one watched but sex in
the backseat accompanied highvolume film score, but she was thought
defective or frightening being so ready, no boy lasted long. she
always told them she loved so they laughed then she laughed also
but there was a mode of guilt they did not come back. she understood
loneliness she said someone to talk to this revealed herself as
dumb sad yearnings despite slut evidence to the contrary even when
cruel, they dropped her off on the main highway ½ mile to walk
down her dirtroad alone 2-3 a.m. she called it lonely, sadness as
if all animals we are comprehensible as one.

before age 17 she was thrice slapped
and punched during sex twice beaten after dropped on the ground
as the car roared off spit gravel in her face once driven out by one
boy to a keg party the desert headlight-lit like a movie set the sole
female 12 males gangfucked vagina anus mouth held down squeezed
hit with bruises everywhere nude her body beer semen vomit smeared
residue of stuporous group dicks her ripped clothes thrown in a
truckbed they drove off leaving darkness she found her way back
crawling the scratchy ditch along the Hwy some number renamed
red spraypaint Paseo Pussy, Calle Puta

of the desert of Time juicy red pulps encircled with hard
pricks(hearts-pierced-by-thorn) appear to succor thirsty masses
oozingGod cum squirt divine juice on the desiccate lost tongue

etc etc her fathers wild spasming from Bibles is always the voice
shes heard. Men are thirsty Men are thirst and hunger she hungered
also but was also generous for sweet distribution of life among
all Comers. for she wandered the desert with Sympathy, a difficult
time every thief a crucifix of bone sex perjury or masturbating
visions but is not seen or prophecy goes in and out skulls of radio
crimes background noise screams turn on and off like water. she
who swallows swords like Pain disdained as one affliction among
many.

she too saw God an enormous gold piston descendent from
the sky a furious drill shining and spinning this gilt spin into
her belly which her flesh closed around spasmodically and muscles
clencht facilitating the red hot corkscrewing motion until she
spurted exploded forth all wealth(in matter) in command of her
imagination.

as if Earth mined, it worked in her mysterious ways. a
girls soft earnest heart is terrible Genital of darkness. when
people know it was one of the hearts wounds sex organs of god they
are not shattered by it. a pilgrimage will be made(someday), to
touch the abhorred(all over her) as proof of Something

then there was his room alone smell of semen. small bed
hotplate table chair a closet toilet 4 walls. the unusual wallpaper
a dark red expression stained black ink figures classically drawn
fleshy nudes fat women reclined spilled breasts hips thighs around
3 walls and behind refrigerator. all these look like his mother the
religious one she waited 67 years to be 'lifted up' but died flat
on her back stopped heart inside pendulous white jellymound. beside
bed and over the ceiling seemed continuation of this but on closer
look other things babies boys girls ripped and pasted porno pages
dildoes cocks sucked widespread vaginas a rapine wallpaper to
scream and come into your eyes at sleepless night.

he lived here, on little
money doing odd jobs. sinkbowl of scummed dishes food scraps
greasy water and glue brushes in a mayonnaise jar. on the table a
stack of pencil sketches perfectly unoriginal plump nudes '50s
pinups womens faces with pageboy hairdos smiling at him offering
themselves like Coke. while drawing his other hand pulled at his
dick then the pencil dropped with both hands he came ejaculation
smell then mixed with just-washed hands some cheap male cologne

tv on orangecrate flickering a game of couples doing things, the
sound turned down
he called himself cowboy, he never rode a horse except
6 years old a mechanical pony outside a drugstore with a stolen
quarter. this became model of Desire. he called his car a mustang
it wasn't it had a rearing plastic stallion with a huge dick where
others had a Madonna or hula dancer on the dashboard.
few or no friends, visitors for as they
said if you walked in his door he'd shoot you with bad dream
bullets. not a real cowboy or man but who knew what else, to be
avoided. he dressed like a childs paperdoll, hat boots levis
longsleeved shirt bandana attached to a flat image one-dimensionally
with tabs, no rounded body. he couldnt see it this way but felt
something, people anywhere eyes swept over him like dustmops then
dropped away shaking off lint or dust he hated them but knew what
they didn't. for a small man he was big as a horse when he stuck
it to a woman he felt that way, not often, it seemed that big when
he masturbated with his eyes open the dark room only a naked
Penthouse open a poster of pussy spread over the ceiling above
his eyes and the exploding come it seemed even bigger because he
wasn't, 5'7" skinny body no chest narrow head geeky big ears pinched
face, nature was not kind so he didnt forgive women for nature
his mother or any slit despising him. or schoolkids beating him
like a girl but this was not the time to think about it.
among every reptile of the desert crawling poison snakes
scorpions anything they could to photograph fuck famous cowboys
celebrities with big dicks he wore the hat the boots nothing
else while jacking off gazing at the wallpaper.Could see hard tips
of brown boots extending from his nose, the dick the boottip,
beyond them the Moon fat on the mountains nude juicy their rumps
up humping the western mountains white come on tits come straddling
invisible horses huge studs their slits rubbing wet leather saddles
cunt slimey hair the boottip enters shaved naked girl pussy
other countries theyre sold for it, even babies ugly
cripples bad things done on videos hurt fuck kill chop up bought
with ordinary dollars population control he was no different,
pervert, nature did it first everywhere. little indian girl
disappeared from the alley by the river found 2 days later cut
open, the arroyo, no one would know who does things too many of
them, they were already dead. grind up for dog food without doubt
like horses were, but cheaper than horses in those places. women

dripped with diamonds pearls rubies cut little baby cunts, cold as
ice could buy things milk bread blankets vitamins medicine clothes
school(the energy of dirty things more necessary than food or
good thoughts) but they didnt care it was them, whores, the real
rapers sucky red mouths and cunts everywhere wearing their cuts out
all over the place deserved a slaughter.
                                  an American, could do anything if
rebalanced nature. he felt penises as highways no speed limit
into the horizon spread open at his will his will was his dick his
boot on the gas pedal into blasting Nothing the Void HOLE he must
make in Nothing with his name on it every billion sperm worming
into it God did it to make everything thats what the hole was for
and what he did his dick steel highway unobstructed desert shaft
no limit of events Eternity was speed of fuck black eruption
volcano beyond light
        only when he paid, it wasnt right no free man should
have to pay for it make them give it free just to be left alive.
aome of the ugliest holes on earth. he liked the ugly ones because
they deserve it. his mother the religious one he can only recall
dead, bloated. he mailordered blowup dolls one in the closet one
in the bed imagine fucking shithole punching her fat face mouth
toothless the rubbery breasts. beyond wallpaper blood dreams
deranged mind of another galaxy rancid lard corpse seeped through
dustslat windows of his eyes before his eyes turn around shot
in the brain groin beg it wont do any good i make the rules shut
up strangle you dick yr hole forever choke on this
        but, couldn't. or make her eyes roll back in her head
with pain, spasms or any way she couldn't look at him, like God
blasting her blind.

so they met at the café some intersection as his finger crossed
with hers like on a coffeemug or trigger, then he shoved it across
the counter in her direction asking for more. she had not noted
him beyond others, except a smell of straw and manure for 2 weeks
hauling fertilizer haybales horsefeed in a ranchers flatbed
parked in the gravel lot in its far corner away from the power
semis.
        from the table in his room he began to sketch on
napkins at the café, positioned first at the counter then a small
rear booth he tried black felt pen it ripped the paper then a

ballpoint pen piling drawings up in stacks then shoved them at
her one by one as she passed or came to pour coffee refills. the
females he drew had nothing to do with her, he attempted animals
but couldnt, he drew a childish valentine heart and then in the
middle of it stab his penknife because that was the way it looked,
red. then he got lost in the essential curve gashed with blood,
buttocks rounded glistening lips on the magazine cover all chocolate
fleshbox then opens itself, not eating shit but he didnt know what
he was drawing now a dozen cupid bodies all with implicit hearts
between their legs, of one sort or another sketched curly black
hairs dense the spewingout crazy with black slashes all over the
cherub body she came to pour coffee and looked at this then his
face then saw on the inside of his right arm near the tender part
of the elbow tattoo of a heart with teardrops falling, it dripped
blood
                          alone to close that night she returned
pie and sandwiches to refrigerator wipe off tabletops and counter,
dishes cups spoons left drying in sanitizer as she did all this he
moved from the rear booth up to the cashregister waiting but never
looked at her she hung apron grabbed wallet lastly shut off the
neon windowsign that never stopped highway or hunger. and it was
easy to edge her out the door as the place closed down around
them he herded her toward the sole vehicle, they walked through
dark without talk. well she is stupid he thought yet her
solidity climbing up into the truck, banging shut her door, even
pointing to the side road leading off into the desert where this
thing was to happen.
                          a place under no moonlight he stopped the truck
got out pulled blanket off the seat, a sage space beyond boulders
not close to rocks rough up the dirt with his boottip snakes red
ants scorpions, he lay the double blanket on cleared ground. she
didnt talk but watched from rim of event horizon. he knew the
routine her insect eats male fucking chews swallows his head as
sperm squirts drops on female receptors sex equals death for
cowboys but not this time he was planning no bugs no prisoners
either everything changed when he was the man. theres a hole theres
a gun theres a knife theres a woman one begins one ends nothing
criminal gods law except he didnt believe in god except he's like
me, no sucker. he did not move to kiss her or undress her she was
removing her blouse and skirt and underpants he wanted to push
her on her knees while he stood over her stuff her mouth

barbara mor

but she lay on the blanket naked he had to undress
he didnt like to be watched she took something for granted that
was stupid and some insult to him trying to get personal into his
head so he removed his shirt his belt but kept his levis, boots
he unbuttoned his jeans and dropped to the blanket over her so
this one deserved a smash everything he'd ever thought
                              love demonizes the human and
humanizes the demon it is somewhere midway between them in a
vast dark beautiful space of gaping openness. knees up her legs
opened she reached her arms around him her small breasts belly
hot too close he shuddered on her flesh for she knew of course
the breaker of men not their sex but their loneliness that is not
female solitude or the great unaccompanied sentient earth but
lostness they begin to weep, grown men(unlike boys reflexive
cruelty) but men as if such sex were long lost souls return to
original home and would shudder choke or weep in this way as
now. he could not dream her experience of men beyond the usual.
how this poor animal has been punished for Being. her sympathy
for the one who must penetrate for the first time the mysteries.
          who actually cries and she presses her hand on the
back of his neck saying I love you Dont cry and often then he
becomes vicious I'll make you cry bitch but this one said nothing
he raised his head from their squirm and sweat he told her not
to look at him, she did not close her eyes but continued naked
and moving her total body up to meet him
                              he was too soft to stay in he
twisted up and from her pulled his pants down below his knees
slipping out the penknife from the pocket placed in dirt above
her head then with both hands he began kneading and hurting her
breasts to get himself hard muttering words mantras of cunt to
conjure pictures while he is fiddling around with her Body the
apertures and anemone juices sucking and drooling his fingers
inward and then stick the twatjuice in her mouth then grab the
penknife open it slice off her nipples and, one in each fist, rub
them into her eyes then stuff them bloody rubbery things up her
cunt and then his hand was wet with everything. violently he spread
her knees and pushed into her spewing words rhythmically as he
screwed his dick around and around in her hole, spit and sweat
dropt from his mouth and glistening face just like fevered saliva
flies from the exalted preachers face and lips she'd seen in the

20

night men are the same in sex and God the lust of belief the lust
of fuck the same lust only one is secret the other out loud. he
was hard he was coming but it didnt stop coming and it all exploded
outward into her eyes
that he is screaming but no sound occurs
he was screaming but no sound occurs rather it enters the pitch
beyond human hearing this is how she sings
ionic wires and buzzard shrieks overhead supercharged electrons
the field that hums transparent air all the way into mountains,
blue ice, cloudy spasms building up swirls of claw and prairieland
badlands forest swamp roads cities all places they had never
been, suctioned into one uprooted vortex. that sensation of the
universe spirals faster and faster the Illusion of Dream of Terror
is(utterly) now and Real, centrifugal his fingers of boots digging
dirt oil erupting his face black sweat huge as God dissolving her
petals centripetally grind downward and inward the funiculus cord
cry tornado louder and greater, expanding shining molecular cunt
walls within her grow the vacuum of everything, exponential
amoeba squid octopi vacuity itself Inside itself implosion of
liquid night lava neurons ecstasy the largest eye in the universe
within her grew the void of God stares inside of depth a darkness
no one can see but it sees.
dismemberment of time(he goes into) great black birds with
whirling razor wings dropt down into his brain rotating vaginal
helicopter blinds him to Now everafter as he is sliced (species
limbs taxonomies)pieces of raw meat to feed into the upward
motors. suckt inside out as if eyelids eyeballs tongue heart gut
lung dick and scrotum more balls all at once revolving skin
sucked into the biggest mouth in a universe of eaters eating eaten
all at once the Worlds of his scrotum and of his eyes, all vision
vacuumed out at once into the black nest of hair and sarcofibers
elementary cosmic strings
her final vacuum death, in a big
swoon to be born again some other dimension or time or microscopic
algae, bacterium dog cockroach swallowed inward into worm realm
maggot fly creeping lizard crawling things extreme of beginning
and pain of matter conscious and tongueless to the end of
infinite Vox and beyond born again and repeated again and again
via this event of Gift of slime generation

and when it was done her dead body nothing but bones
staked spreadeagled on the desert a horizontal crucifixion with
some dry rust blood seeped from where her mouth eyes nostrils
wept from wounds of pelvis and breast but she is not there of her
remaining skeleton a head dragged off eaten as one days meal
den of hungry coyotes
　　　　of him remaining nothing or just a fleck of red bandana
smelling of Vitalis hair oil the discriminate Hole excluded the rest
of him voided so to speak into the uterus beyond speed of spectacle
or dark thought. drops of unanalyzed substance spattered around
which could be tears or blood or engine grease
they came to this place rarely a few the curious
like Jesus almost it was said
but not really

the blue rental

Sea of Hunger

His head was between her legs, something like a flowerbud between
thighs of scissors. A phone was ringing. Indeed, her thighs were steel-
edged, his tongue edgy with blood. Taste of iron petals.
But a phone was ringing.
         His stock broker—
         She. in the midnight hours?
         He: lips, he said.

Karl Marx: "All of our inventions and progress seem to result in
endowing material forces with intellectual life, and stultifying human
life into a material force."
                         1856

so a metal fish in ravenous hours of water   San Diego Fwy south 1:30 a.m.
Jaguar curves down Mission Bay into Baja Peninsula awake and alone red
electric shark among night surge of ferrous feeders   one among many
65mph   his penis between tides of thighs in the black seat   no radio no CD
trance of oceanic silence   neon streakt highspeed submarine chrome fins
blood leaks from the BMW ahead   squid propel with oily tentacles   octopi
drill glasseye into drivers brain   anemones cling to roadside, gas
stations bars cafes suck in soft bodies from crackt shells   clutch

the lethal wheel between hands of water
his father before him his father before him. the Baja coast, eden:
surf fish abalone perfect sand. live lobsters in a bucket 50 cents each.
before the highway unrolled a long desperate tongue from TJ to La Paz.
shacks visible from 2 lane road, colonias locas rigged with rusty bedsprings
truckdoors appliance crates, cardboard and wind. brown butt kids no
diapers no underwear, barefoot kids running goats sheep over rocky
pastures, squirting warm milk into glass jars. below Rosarito Café Lupe
the old couple kills a chicken when you arrive. outside at rickety tables
cerveza and 7Up, the old womans flapping apron scares up a bird
husband grabs, holds the head on a stump, one whack of a small ax. the
headless beast rums around and around in terrible circles until it grows
tired seeking the old life in such a strange world. all blood spurted out,
pluckt chopped tossed in sizzling lard skillet, this happened in the kitchen,
woodstove, handmade tortillas. you were served tacos with your own personal
chicken. he died for our sins. green hills undulate to the sea, lunar
beaches, tidepools of the beginning. when the new highway reached kilometro
50 they were gone. Via Dolares sweeps by leaves all erased in gringo dust

cross the border like any American. better. wave at the Mexican guard.
como vas? salud, jefe! they know his face. almost 7 years San Diego based
software setup any service any business anyway SMALL TECHNICALITIES, Inc.
in fact no questions asked.
                         over the border it is still America. turistas,
Revolucion, highschool boys wetdream tequila blackout chewinggum
putas on every corner age 9 lose yr virginity on a 43 year old bruja roll
down barrio ditch into wet mossbed rank with trash and bottles sleep 5 hours
and awake a virgin, all over and over again. the only sex stink of slimey
green and Dos Equis, because he remembered nothing. beyond the official
line it was still America until the south south south road turns into
another dimension. diagonal into el otro pais. sudden cessation of masks and
neon cocktails. the relentless children sleep 4,5 to a bed, the relentless
night dreams one moon. in the darker suburbs taxis cruise without lights
y las patrullas vienen solo por la muerte, buying or selling. when he
crosses this border his sex changes. one white fish in an ocean of brown
flesh. always the bones loosen, chest belly anus are vulnerable. cinderblock
nations crawl over maps of his body like cockroaches. he became a woman,
haunted by surrender.
                         in this dark he drove by smell. arc slowly west
as if downward to the sea. metallic and cool hunger remember salt air

is blood. shark sensation, he'd been here before. global buyers, arms deals mercenary arrangements, private club on the alta playa, utilities bounties girls. more sinister than the border he passed through 1,2,3 guarded gates the drive curved finally to the entrance of the surreal palacio. a boy took his Jag and he walked into the Life. patio mosaics bougainvillea geranium pink arcades of stone scalloping a central fountain, which was lit like a holy person from inside. the music of rich voices the rich music of voices a ballroom 12 piece band, a few dance, young men amusing wives and daughters of others. around the walls in suits of power los patrones deal. everyone looks good in the glow of electric candelabra

    he finds a table spread with liquor bottles, punch, condiments, glass, ice. a Sonoran mosca mixes drinks drops in mint and lemon with suggestive brown fingers. the godfather is the pope bent over, gaze into a dark mirror of reversals. so his face is the good blond country, innocence by default. he turns around to be introduced, the known voice of Lopez, Tijuana rug merchant, or friend of his father Verrano border realestate of the old days. here we are again, when green hills rolled to the sea etcetera. tidepools thick with exotic creatures. Verranos hands fanned wide. we're still here, guero! Lopez flashed gold but his eyes always swam as prey. the woman moved in on him, someones deal closer. a tall gringa, 40 plus too tan too flaca, she maneuvered him around the room kalaidescope of glistening fed flesh, naming names he didnt need to know, her cigarette and highball smoking in one hand.
then a famous name, a stunning mezcla, her american father
nearby. the gringa leaned into him, selling or buying, and the daughter who is Sylvia, smiles. old news photos of electric prods running shoes burning tires the Zombi chases nubile blonde thru black trash alleys she escapes, good footware. Tonton Macoute. el padre gets in his life the result of what he creates with 'only images.' this midnite flower, born to love/power. her Brazilian soapopera mother dies in a fiery planecrash on location in Venezuela, nasty divorce or narcotraffic, some C. American druglord/politico pissed with failed PR campaign. caught on film, the stars explosion backgrounds sad/romantic funeral sequence. the daughter had her mothers dark gold looks but taller, smarter.
introductory words a cleancut opportunistic allAmerican boy, and now they are joking about voodoo dolls
this is true says Sylvia. baseballs and Cabbage Dolls both made in Haiti $2.50 day wages 60,000 workers. and their little cachuchas! exploited or saved? you tell me. they love America
i could sell 60,000 hackers

such people hack with machetes. we not only clean yr toiletbowl we make
yr toiletpaper. and yr douche spray. and yr vibrating finger up yr ass.
we know you so well. we watch you on tv
she could deliver serious news on Telemundo. warm hands slid another
cold drink in his hands. he described his operations, chaos control
keeping the lid on Disaster apocalypse systems plagues riots freetradezones
e-coli world melons workers squat shitting in fields no facilities genetic
damage engineered health clusters organmarkets shift via liberal birth
spacing anorexia Ebola child dictatorships. your hard problem our
soft solution. SMALL TECHNICALITIES. need my company.
well, a man glanced one glass eye. i hope you are in good company.
small is beautiful. bueno, si. as for me I want only one big thing said
Sylvia. there was a flash of light, many teeth glasses raised among
glittering thoughts and her swimming shoulders.

then lights and
music dim, a hush of oxygen. all turn and Sylvia expresses everyone
in one sigh. on a dais in the middle of the room a long lavish blonde lay
nude her creamy arms flung above her head, thick yellow waves of hair
wild growth the nausea of tendrils overflowing the deeply red plush
chaise longue. either side, 2 naked brown children ages 4-5 one boy one
girl each clutched one full breast in small hands, they kneeled sucking
as if milk did come from their golden mother. her eyes half closed her
body carelessly tossed with a kind of fishnet now you see erotically
everything now you dont as she shifts a massive thigh and pelvis, between
her legs a youth, slim and dark, short hair, bare chest, tight beach trunks,
wrists cuffed held behind his back by a very heavy pockmarked policia
tan shirt pants gunbelt, 2 others move to pull her thighs wide open
the boys face shoved down into the wet gold cunt, stink of games and
hunger   Eat, hijo! la comes! may all enjoy!
el mundo consumes 75 million barrels of oil daily. how much cunt,
vato? how much tuna!
jefe from behind squeezed his shoulder. one glass eye man it seemed
was Lopez' brother
pues, these ninos perform well, buen faena. we send them home
with bellies. esta muy simpatico, hombre.

some hallucinogen dropped in his drink, magic in the club water. the
daio seemed slowly turning, then his cellphone rang he turned around like
a dog inside his brain but couldnt find the answer. Sylvia stood before
him, sudden extension of the dizzy tableau. Can you feel the pulse of the

the blue rental

world, she murmured, more than drunk, close, her breasts and thighs moved
against him. Life is good, huero guero. babies born blind still smile. babies
born deaf, they laugh! she didnt miss a beat. a drink in each hand, she
kissed and licked his cheeks, one side the other, lipstick or blood. he took
his glass then free arms wrapped around each other warmly they seemed
to dance. she was almost as tall as he, he could hear the seas voice in
the whorls of her ear
you know the Georgian mother, Russian I mean. yes, he knew of it.
when she went to the hotel with her 8 year old daughter, so poor so crazy
with poverty! the bathtub was already packed with ice. she sold the
girl alive, to 2 men. immediately they took la mozuela into the bathroom,
slit her throat, extracted the organs right there, fresh. she paused to
kiss him deeply on the lips. but think! certainly the buyer from the
Caucasus mountains, the Caucasian gentleman that is, he paid for a
childs organs, no? child size! surely they were meant for his own child?
a beloved son or daughter, o nieto. in the end, an act of love, yes? we must
consider the whole picture, el globo. todo el mundo, siempre. her face
nuzzled into his neck she hummed
all horror as a form of love, he considered
the reverse was certainly true
then her eyes open glistening, acts of discovery.
but as we've just seen, el pobre y la rubia, it is eating itself that is
awful, don't you think? her white teeth unbelievably neat. el sexo is so
innocent and sharing. but to eat, we are among the beasts, carnivores.
i'm hungry he said, nibbling on her lobe.
eating is cannibalism
surprise me
to the side of the room, slanted like dos borrachos, long tables platters
dishes bowls half replenished with fresh items half plundered by the
feast. guests stood around still talking, snacking, some chewed on the
genitals of adolescent girls, filleted, human fingers they were gnawing
the joints pickled and anonymous. there were ears boys testicles
nipples an international variety of dips and sauces. 2 plates napkins
forks she turns from the extravaganza she offers on a cracker between
her fingers aimed seductively at his mouth what looks like newborn
vulva, the labia spread with bluish crème paste
pate of baby girl eyeballs $2000 for brown $2500 for the rarer blue
blue like his
she leans forward flicks her shining lizard tongue into his mouth
your own personal taco

he would recross the border at dawn before that time
unwind the road out of a dream, the chemical night. always it had
flowed in one direction a gradient FULL to EMPTY dependable as money but
now at the end the flow reversed, mysterious Alive a periodic slimemold.
return to America as if a tsunami followed him, loomed up inside his
rearview mirror of Visions.
he knows he will awake one day find everything being removed in
bodybags. or there is no direction in the sea
because isnt this what it wants, to drown dissolve itself in the instant
ocean. immune boundaries permeate and destroy once and for all, DESIRE,
the plasm of One. the tube film neon eyes boombox beat it into yr
skin. one among many. torsos flanks gray naked shoulders and brain
revolving slowly northward through watery lanes, 20 100 1000 tides of
8 billion fish flesh needling into some punctured shore or border.
to just rest, surrender name identity account into the spreading stain
of the world. inside beyond a luxury to lie back become amoeba all over
the magnified body with no face. Tijuana and dawn. going north was not
going home. he was a spine inside a sea of evolving objects of dreams

but who had known there would be so much acute flesh. bones like knives
stuck out of doorways, ribs elbows pelvic shivs of revengeful hunger
bellies not soft, voluptuous, they were murderous. a conscious shark in the
thick sea. so many nostrils gullets anuses body holes without distinction
sex dinner and murder as the same act. where you cross the borders of
Distance, where bodies go in and out of each other
that all civilizations are only different positions in the sexual act
of one giant melticellular organism continuously fucking feeding
reproducing consuming excreting itself. cf that Frenchmans
pseudopods
             waste and redundance. the great feast
workers rapists slaves abandoned babies the pope the pentagon the
presidents twat a ring of children dancing in a park who just
disappear
so what did they want of him. they would send him to school.
of what. fish?
but can you feel no sorrow for the world

but all this is for the american guest.
hls lntentlons as always are only good
he crosses thresholds to eat, consume hunger. returns followed by
starvation and appetite. export and import. supply and demand. demand

and demand. germs dope seeds women children microcosms sanddollars
biochips electric shoes spleens cameras toxic lotteries mudslides
theres a job, at this party, for a caterer. one who feeds needs to eat
need not be eaten. who did sharks? orcas, the sea itself. nothing small.
his mind enjoyed playing with metaphors but the fact was, glancing at
day coming in the windows, he was young cleareyed useful and very clean
when shaven. corruption in the beholders eye, he could see none. this
is the genius of the american face. you learn in a sea of foreign eyes who
see necessary evil day and night in each other, it is their fact of life.
this ancient scenario was not his. one older brother a San Diego court judge,
sisters married into hotel chains and Hollywood cosmetics. there was
nothing he could not do to achieve more and more then speed away
into the technicolor sunrise. son of gods of good intentions, didnt we
pave all these highways

the border was stuck, both directions
a ricochet zone of uptight fish. for miles and miles into tundra north
down through debris of the Southern Cross, inexorable traffic of workers
and consumers. barely awake, already pissed. agglutinated strangers
waiting for something to move. no frontier at all but a bursting
corridor a rush to the bridal death chamber each wills for the other.
one radio station, bilingual and loud.
yes it is all from Love. murder. merger.
he could not speed forward, or reverse or dream
ooze like sludge into alta california. the pragmatic effects of america.
a rusty lovely pallor of urban morning, some kind of cartoon takes
itself seriously. a skyline with teeth chews up famous names   red spit
in asphalt like an accident   license plates read DEATH, every combination
of numbers dredged up from the sunken night   classic Tacitus, VENALIA
CUNCTA pornographically the billboards are smiling   big metal fish eat
little metal fish, factorial wombs on all horizons spawn efficiently more
and more   if you slow down the mouth behind engulps you whole   and the
mouth behind that is a huge wave full of everything thats been
and the mouth ahead of him and the mouth beyond that

he wondered if he should stare into it   or choke   or swallow

barbara mor

the blue rental

oasis

All moist life is inside now. Dark oases of banks, hotels,
restaurants, avid hearts. Valves open, glass doors sluice
heavily inward all hours day and night vegetal interiors
-- we are consumers. Sudden biologic air light water.
Tendrils of machinery alleviate the body, green plants florescent
liquids circuitries of oxygen nutrients through skins of semi-
human buildings, tubes wires electric cells inside walls
pump what is left of earth from a deep place into our
veins. From the ice of mental systems into our final
thoughts
       Terrariums, aquarium fish enjoy the same
ambience (if plunged in a desert of fire, enact careers
on the surface of Mars). This is how it feels.
       Clocks, all coordinates of time and space
intersections of philosophy metallurgy famine sex
become this place. Watery exchanges of money, historic
lips hands palms genital intellect and soft pulses of
bodies doing business. Little sweats of laughter. Your

interchangeable face
      Almost among rainforest of planters wooden
boxes automatic drip salad bars, euphoric negative ions
stainless coffee coca chrome. Something feeds, that
mysterious gut. Deliver us, from thirst from depths
complex artificial suckt and pumped Inside terminal
flesh; breathe see swallow urine spit shit (even us).
      This is how bodies are kept alive

a girl works here junction StMarys Interstate 10 open
24/7 burger hotdog cheese fries egg&sausage muffin bagels
microwave and deepfry racks of jumbo platter dawn
noon midnite factory preprepared coleslaw jello bun
boxes coffee 3 sizes drinks straws napkins salt&pepper
sugar mustard catsup relish tomato salad onions
floor mop the drink bar spills of icetea cola fresh salad
bar spray plants wipe tables ice crush supply smile
locals and travelers there are no seasons directions hours
breakfastlunchdinner one continuous hunger & thirst
the fire of flesh(day)the electric night
                              they enter
from air so thick it is swallowed, dust oil saliva
craving coke, cherry pie. a simulation of clarity the
friendly menu of comfort a desert mirage as target
tattooed on the inside of eyelids
                        so one begins
working midnite to 8 shift then switch, days at the speed
of skills a job low wages tips but cool air almost fresh
scenery paycheck minus meals uniforms (olive/pink)
supplied 2 bathroom breaks w/dehydration
To service and maintain.
          a pilgrim film crawls station to station bloody
appendages the terrible mileage truckers salesmen
insomniac killers all one road give them water some
do not afford airconditioning some do not sleep inside
the world,inferno dreams walk thru doors sweating various
scenarios unlimited caffeine,fluorescent refills the family
in the next booth will not survive the next horrible hour
of our journey enjoy yr food an ancient swamp once

squatted here alkies junkies almost tetrapods lone demented
types who talk to Death foam at the mouth who fornicate
trees These are characters you don't need to know as
they are soon gone. Mormons students wheelchair
bagladies Those who exchange body fluids for rent Those
who exchange body parts for God there is one trained
in junglewarfare carries knives inside him hisses&writhes
about killing something. pimps and other primeval
forces deploy this thought
                                    it is all contained in
ambient light, you are serene among the carnivore
teeth of extinct species splashed on walls, faces of their
instant children who do not emerge from cars,uteri,the family
foodpack squeals and runs among us Patrons must
believe they are served workers must strive to exist for
all come and go and feed and disappear a new girl
sponges up red pieces. become familiar unit among,eons
biotropic units then personnel change another who looks
the same then another and another a boy seems similar
a girl a boy the interchangeable diets of meat except
one is yellowhair then black then brown or taller or plump
or severe behind glasses now and then
To serve and clean
if it is a Theater of cruel things, animal shrine
ritual gut center of world imploding by Doom it feeds
those who enter something nicer than money,the
repetitions of death in happy colors. outside windows as
magnified eyes see dinosaurs of hot steel crush everything
collapsingAges of Destruction reputed urban landscape
between ozone moon asphalt grief video hell,the
air stinks w/corpse perfume terminal gases motors
grind structures night & heat, a molarous grinding of
monstrous machine hearts pumped by terror,blood
thick from the Sun as if edible
                            as meat to mouth, butchers to
confessionals,to bathroomstall hands in common sink(as
a woman paid to comprehend) the distraught flesh
enters. stands in line. it selects it pays. *peccavi*
our serious crimes of romance job shirtsleeves guilty
fingernails let us sit to escape absolve of bad dream
plastic cubicles ruminate last meal before the sentence of

void
       (one may approach patrons wearing fantasies,
garterbelt slit panties whips & leather nothing.
masturbation,or could be eaten for dessert. or 2
businessmen between bankdeal lunch strangulation
orgasm. erotic, of a desert. sacred compared w/
otherwise it feeds,eats who enters & will return to,some
snake tendon slips from walls & slithers into groins
of,who feed the monsters beyond of,markets traffic chewing
Eschaton   all one thing
     and Look, beyond the window they look beyond the
window suddenly minds explode in jet planes they
tumble in fire Look bodies ignite the sky essential *Numa* is
leaking.And black angels swoop the rapturous birds
hook out pieces Look the god eats the world
     This is news,headlines. Natl EnquirerAZStarUSAToday
was yesterday last month reruns from the year before
kept stackt on tables for those restless for time (here is
no time   )
It is true human pain feeds spirits devis demons the
circling maw of Consciousness.red print streams on
flesh pulp,over&over like a radio scream in all their
stereo cellphone skullboxes No one hears this music
                                        the tabloids are
neatly folded and stacked on front tables, but who
opens or who reads

       the menu spread upon the table the blind one reads
w/his fingers. sopas ensaladas the toenails of absent
monkeys. El Ciego on one side of the booth El Oculto opposite
past midnite for many hours the dishes between them
glow & quiver w/jewelled putrescence,as of maggot pearls
of meatfeasts gorged 500 years b4. uno del dedo del pie.
crow pie. blood pie. pisada pie. El Ciego squeezes mustard on
his final hamburger & El Oculto considers the varieties of sweet
deserts. as brujos see it,shit tubes sewers niagaras of urine&
above all pain,the carcass hangs from the ceiling&screams.thus
Paco y Flaco enjoy the company of the world this axis mundi
revolving
       ah Tlaltecuhtli chinche. big Ozone hole swallows up

the blue rental

Brazil. i can taste Brazil. 1000 rebel elephants machinegunned
in Kenya. hey they can GMO yr kids to be Human Bombs.
Local news, chickens cats dogs ninos flayed sacrificially
splayed on 11th Ave traintracks. that is in the neighborhood.
a local beauty who collects the hearts of men? he reads
headlines or menus of ritual remains as the cartperson
bends nearby to clear dishes,a blonde new body. he makes
her laugh. mira, dice: Our Mother, huge ugly Toad skin
pustles of staring eyes elbows ankles knees wristbones bloody
mouths croaking Feed me! Feed me! tu madre. Y tambien the Sun,
he eats too
                    the girl does not know if he sees or truly
lives in darkness,wearing dark glasses at midnight the burnt
retinas of his partner sometimes spin like tornadoes they
share between them one white stick w/ruby knob. Poco
thin in jeans white t-shirt Loco even skinnier sometimes a
baseball cap looking backward. they ate everything,everything
one dish after another back to the table never sated never fat
they ate all night. clowns to nightworkers, a rapid
turnover
Those old people fed the Sun
corazones humanos,wrapt in warm tortilla flesh
ancient Mesoamerican fastfood: burritos por El Dios
a brown thumb jerks at the outside mirage, 4am parkinglot
crouched before dawn neon smog pulsed in blackbeats of unslept
cars. Gringos feed god farts. Talk about a religion
Tonan, Our Mother, w/many wiry dirty fingers he taps the
table, they could be spiderlegs. what does She eat? Creature
excrement menstrual blood raw placentas corpses. dump
all this good food in the toilet, guero. rivers oceans it becomes
water. Pocho stares into his Coke. i think i'm drinking it
no wonder She croaks
the girls body appears at the table, he leans & deeply
sniffs her crotch. no sangre de las flores,relojes de la luna
no iron no sulfur no ammonia no chemistry between you
pero bugspray,no morbid bodies! his fingers go in&out of her
in strange ways,the starving maggots. organs lockt in cans cars
antidecomposition boxes,UR coffins. Ocho very excited now
digs Bic from levi pocket clicks openLight flares upward thru
his skull becomes an owl reverse ocelot,fountain of Death.
the girl stares & smiles. this dialog between them quantum

tlachtli faster than light she like many others mildly retarded
yet cheerful therefore. from the top of his head come fireworks,
Nuclear explosion
my girlfriend the Witch ate my heart w/her eyes.or,just looking,
she can chew off yr leg muscle, no pain,you just fall over. is
that nice?
no counting for Taste
speaking of waist, la cinga,news item Aug 02: the Equator
circumference is growing. The world is fat
eats too much junk
speaking of justice,his finger sibylically moves upon the
air, Bovine Spongiform Encephalopathy,a chronic wasting disease.
todo el mundo is wasted. i have dumps in my head of dead
species,upsidedown extinct little toenails & babyeyes.maybe it is
these cannibals,his fingers fluttering many unseen knives fly out
embed surrounding neurons of eaters. Bovas Sponges Encephalants,
mis hijos! revenge of bushmeat
after all it is not brain surgery
do you believe in poetry?
a mute exchange of stares thru black mirrors, the smoke
curling up from somewhere they have no cigarettes,then
Chuyo y Puyo laugh it is a very dry laughter like snake
rattles behind a rock in the arroyo
In 1536 Cabeza de Vaca y 3 companeros crawl delirious from
this desert back in Sinaloa bullshit their homey slavers re
7 cities of gold I saw them in El Norte
1540 Coronado goes after the gold of Cibola
Mr Head of a Cow Senor Cowhead who hallucinates civilization
from a shitpile
Cibola is a softdrink i think

dawn nears,Cholo y Polo alternate rising up approach the
saladbar fill bowls w/lettuce radish pepper onion ovary
battery amygdala (all you can eat)word salad. one person
mops one wipes racks one stacks dishes sterilized to receive
the 5th Sun. it is black cool empty as the world will ever be.
they munch as cattle greens fall from their mouths Chui thrusts
his 44oz supercup across the table. More, bottomless thirst
I must be dead. a green fluid pours in from the machine
air,Slice or 7Up. Louie picks thru many plates of extinct

chicken,Who nibbled on all the bones? he waves 10 centuries of
fingerbones at the girl,thus pulled to their table. greasy
Quetzalcoatl in the underworld let ghosts chew our ancestors
huesos so the new world born from them is denied immortality
a bucket of bones chewed like rats or dog spirits, comprendes?
and That is why you must die
a trance of not knowing what they do,Chui delicately floats
exotic dishes before her eyes.a saucer heapt of little tongues&
sugar. bowls of dreams&ears.a platter of spongy crazy thoughts.
you deserve this! her eyes glaze over a fragment of time flutter
& then she laughs.pulse in her throat,Pinga y Chinga reach out
tap to the beat her hand surrendered palm up on the table. or
her spine as she leans over a well of drowned flesh,crumbs
There are so many girls,let us choose one
She has a good heart. moist & cheery

> *our village in Sonora where the central plaza horno is kept*
> *hot,the old woman w/many sons in various places*
> *over under near around south of the border who knows*
> *what they do the midnite trucks pull into town,it is*
> *said the bodies are already cut into reasonable small parts*
> *she further chops some grinds some knead into maiz y*
> *flor tortillas big pots of chili carne seca the horno is*
> *so hot it disposes of everything some smashed bones and*
> *useless gristle incinerate of course*
> *   but no waste of good meat the*
> *reputation grows you know what you are eating vato,yes*
> *the ritual lunch,and who says only gringos are serious for*
> *recycling*
> *Consumers are consumed*
> *have you heard the serpent eats his own tail*
> *he gets indigestion*

      dripping night, hearts other working organs exit
bodies of eating patrons Dew or Squirt rain from air into the
extra large cups. El Ciego y El Oculto their visages frogs
reptiles insects sudden tongues flicker out forkt&crackling
curl back poisonous w/tasting,warty eyes erupt their body
skins echinoderm and styrofoam. agents of fire,gila
or salamander each dawn enter the sacred terribleOutside melts
them together obsidian&silver,some impossible alloy,as

dining utensils & surgery they return to autopsy night
inside this Mind,system of in&out species architecture
franchise agony w/hallucinated appetite doors open&close,you
fill you empty the larger Hunger surrounds this datum
is Unknown placental machinery hung from jet hooks
overhead who grinds and twists in a voids pain
enact our search for the magical body
here one hurls a self into Dawn splits open horizons
of heat,as Nanahuatl the ugly diseased w/sores white chalk
dusted & pasted soft feathers BigChicken leaps into That
rotisserie making the 5th world,or any suicide bomber
dumb girl or this chica w/the bone wagon
meat fruits ah cooked or raw little pink bird revolves on
the spit her marinated members
he whispers this while squeezing small breasts w/mystic
hands inserts 2 fingers deep up her cunt swirling vaginal
juices pushes into her lips for a taste smells of everything
you do to live accumulate sez Pinga quoting somebody
in her ecstasy,white jiz &plumes to be consumed alive
molten pearl eyes squealing animal shit cages of Terror
barbecue heroic young flanks & virginal bellybutton,toes
claws hooves knuckles clutcht in escape wires she almost
screams but it sounds like hideous cattle. eating faces
leer upward into her skeleton the offered organ becomes
the Sun like a bursting aorta or flower, do you
think she circles back into soft drink fluids triple bun
meat meals the sponges of weeping cows
hung from hooks the bodies the priest w/blood clots stinking
his hair quipu knots of yr black jello,the butcher plungd
into yr brain in the end huge blotting out All the heart
extracted carcass tumbles endlessly down stone levels one body
tumbling forever over & over or many one upon another zombi
glyph of our Despair.human lines move to eat the execution
weekend special serpentine of lard sweating Fear moisture
to maintain a certain order sez Pinga y Chinga not that it
needs any help they pick their mutual teeth savor slow
food of the Otherworld succulent jewel intestine of wild
things Thought that knows it is a dream,stew of jaguar
rump & swamp jaw,quetzal w/crushed ice salad of
jungular fire

the blue rental

* * * * * * * * * * * *

    horizon is a border a line the shimmering mirage
water from which arises Eye of God a periscope tall oracular
spine turns all directions slowly no Thing escapes
Mexico/US Nogales to Nogales the eyebeams lock on each
other the Future someone is watching the footprints appear
mysterious the margins of pages,desert jungle mountain
track LaVenta Tlapallan Xibalba Mictlan (in 9 days)
they descend from stars & time into yr historys calendar,a
bowel highway Yucatan/Sonora invisible among the
crawling bellies,the flies the thirst scorpions migrating
suicide, the footprints hallucinate themselves into
existence Guatemala Michoacan Naco in 9 days the
footprints walk across the checkpoint detached from
a body and then there are 2,men made of sticks scratch
scratch upon sand,asphalt one dressed in a suit the other
a mustache drooping cigarette the beam on his cane sweeps
out sensating ancient radio voices Tucson mariachi in 9
days, 2 moscas appear a street in time space,raiment of
jeans white t-shirts very clean they assist the Sun

now flowers here,that can no longer Be(exude) in the
worlds Nature, cool museum environs Commerce & giant
morgues Meso pyramids w/bodies tumbling Tombs of Credit
& Desire,the footprints arrive *hearts murder intersection*
via crusht rock gulpt sand the mystic centuries our
most perfect children flayd alive the billboards splasht
in dead eyes gods colossal hunger,cross boulevard pass
over stone ruins endtime landscape chainlink razorwire
instant parking lot surrounding Paradise,2 stickmen
dressed in flesh leap poison & rust,arrive in trance
ENTRANCE th'excavated Earth .a mall of Waters,green
vines fountains of butterflies the lucid merchandise,ionic
air of purchased bodies going places up&down solely as of
a Mind,the translucent cylinders (what contains us

& what we contain) mezzanine eruptions of food,drink
horrific imagination Here we are speak 2 stickmen not
lost in a crowd Mannequins rise on escalators from
a deep sea naked & singing,ecstatic packages of seahorse
coelacanth coral the exploded ears of great whales
Mesozoic treasures for every taste, silent holes open over
all the white sleeping dream babies,mammals & fish the
commodities arrive depart yr jade eyes, boxes shelves
continents of sacred things shiningly wrapt & severed from
their roots of Meaning,nuestros muchachos carry little
scissors for manicure purposes the red fingernails of delicious
women swallow'd w/delirious oceans,tidal acetones &
gut swirls purges of all things arms legs consumer torsos
faces words Designers&Appliances Everything up from
the Basement dripping immaculate fatality,they open
fat cardiac wallets toss agony around like money,Shop
of the Dead on the last day, *buy buy*, blood pours from
their ears in unfathomed pressures
      Tlaltecuhtli a monstrous Toad,SAPO whose entire body
stares back w/unblinking eyes, 10 thousand eyes &mouthholes
croak for blood,now she is a fountain in the mall, mira, 50
feet tall what sprouts from her many mouths is a fluid,red,&
the children want to play in it climb all over her as mothers
hunt for shoes & kitchen knives,they slip in the viscous bubbles
& pink foam in their nostrils,spun candy,they jump&splash in
violet jets,wherever 2 stickmen walk war erupts on video
screens more screaming children Pancho y Luncho open a
mouth to scream, bejewel'd & perfum'd her cosmetics mixt
w/corpse ash menses scorpion pheromones crusht mantis
eyes & ectopic waste, they smear the magnetic body w/
star paste our mad poetic ones become shining flesh
as lipstick erupts on every stoppt face lingerie w/eels &
strangled necks
      Condensed by fire the human body is
40-50 diamonds pure carbon of yr loved ones one for every
finger w/every finger they enter all things as burglarize a
body filch raw thought scoop out a cunt or 2 eyes
(remember they are blind)the unzipt skins purpose slithers
away tap tap on bone & people gaze back a Time fragment,flutter
& laugh when it laughs flickerd split tongue claws curld quik
on escalator rail or beadpurse or a shoulder as one leans over

a table rippling bright scarves sandals underwear or cameras
w/nictitating lenses (remember they are 2 sticks)
gods azteca appear,converse but soon grow bored that is
Hungry only on these terms did we live herd animals w/
tasty dreams what dies horribly & becomes yr flesh what
gods lick & swallow from sleep & death, monkeys pygmies
many famous people Elvis Diana Jesus Selena calf flayd
as its mothers eyes in the Church of Eating the people
swell up the gods swell up you look out windows they are
filling up the sky passionately sublime flesh eaten on tv,
snackfood torture rooms motel organ fiesta why is earth
ballooning w/pain it is not junk food senor it is God Flesh
Carne Dios fat w/terror all the hot sex slaughter so all
will Eat Glory vicarious deity cannibalism of course this
is culture. as Everything lives by eating the Sun,the Sun is
hungry too, why not, long red fingers thru glass grab &
break open ripe skulls,baby seeds, good intentions, gangs
of tongues & acids invade yr openings w/boiling appetite
all moisture of the body brain poetry suckt up long tubes
into their noses,the gods snort time fear beauty nothing else
works for eternity all is food & hunger mas y mas y mas
says the Stick & it is not fulfilled

    Mesozoic   (here,beyond) dinosaurs of heat crush
pavements,their evolving & extincting great mouthsof fire
& oil devour smaller things a mechanics of combustion of
everything between ocean & mountain,sky & inward Hell
night & day consumption of rage consuming air of burning
flesh & copal
there is no relief
triumphant glass asphalt metal melded together,orbits
beyond earth melded to earths core helicopters pissing fire
cars trucks buses corpses swollen rotting inside,blowup dolls
w/open mouths, if there were scavengers coyotes vultures
to eat stench from bones but no relief   Cement grinding
motors gun explosions family brains spewn out on freeways
or merciful deep fat fry or skeletons of white dust at
their prayers
a river that runs backward & is always dry,a goddess &
her dark lover coild in each others loins as cosmic dust

Santa Cruz currents of sinews of their love Ontlaqualque *they*
ate the earth Aztec oath to utter truth touch earth w/hand
lick off what clings   as Moctezuma gave to those
conquistadors who disembarked,a mark of respect   &
dragons uncoil to eat unborn babies,spawn of a blood
red woman drunk on blood the Son appears w/swords in
his mouth to slay his enemies & eat them
It grows hotter redder air more red in eye,fire crackles
every atom of breath as it inexorably expands blood pressure
skulls clenched & swollen rage of hearts of course there is
a flutter in the head as all things realize: it is impossible.
To live.

2 stick men in a parkinglot thus crazed by vision w/
stink of all this go into Night luminous w/fire in search of
monstrous answers in search of monsters who can answer
        2 stick thin men,thin as snakes so desperate as
shadows of rats fingernails,the penis of a line, only 2
as naked men running back & forth in th'emptied night, I
offer up body pieces food lungs livers genitals we carry them
in paper sacks, cardboard boxes plastic containers doggybags
for the gods,who offer to north south east west to the
growing voracity of the Sun. or earth moon stars anything
to listen still hungry to live but it is impossible

HERE : a small history of a mining town in the American southwest
(Warren/Bisbee AZ 1985)

No strange thing can happen here. A silence, a slowness of
metabolism that can only replicate itself, nothing strange. A silence,
an accommodation to stillness that exists nowhere else in the world
today, because a world is continuously escaping the silent implications
of here. Some escapes are made possible by the speed of light. Some
become red dots of revolution, or television, which move at the
velocity of consciously dreaming blood. Then there are the slow crawls
of the hungry, some refugees from this place, prodded by a mass
scattering of bullets, along whose trajectories only a few thin souls
can move with imagination. Bullets do not lie in the dust like dried
bread crusts, or shriveled bodies, but deflect. And this is their
strangeness.
      Locations no longer escaping are cemeteries. But they have
found an old way of being.
      Here, however, is a new way. The new mode of being not strange.
      It begins, with roads introjecting from civilizations and deserts,
the asphalt pavement cracked and potholed and strewn with black
rubbery skins shed by snakes. Rolling hills surrounding the town are

blood-red, sparsely clumped with pale green bushes. Roads approach
from all directions, though untraveled, like parched gray tongues
through the hills and entering the town, sinking down to its center,
blistered and graveled with their thirst. It is a quiet hometown place,
simply, with traditional frame and brick houses facing traditional empty
streets, the sidewalks warped and uplifted by heat and the pressure of
something. Because its original builders were bachelor miners, the
homes tend to be small, one and two story in narrow lots, with the
obligatory dull bushes and small trees struggling outward in the traditionally thirsty yards; or, as now, that pale green vegetation, spiked
with lunoid cacti and poppy-thistle. Traditionally, the inhabitants
do not appear on the streets, due to the blaze of heat. A few emerge
to sit on front porches as the evening cools; they are almost entirely
old, retired folk, whose skins are tired of casting off.

Now and then, along a block, a younger household moves in. The
spiky plants are dug out, replaced with sandboxes and swings, and then
children's voices, thin and prickly as the ex-plants, can be heard as
though far off, inside the overwhelming silence of the air. For the
most part, residents are old, and stay inside; or they back their automobiles from garages slowly, glinting in sunlight, and drive inside
these cars from place to place along the scarred streets, like soft and
pale bugs moving inside metallic exoskeletons. Carriages of chitin, in
fact, which, in this town, are traditionally kept in the best condition,
clean, tuned, free from all dents or blood.

Down one side of each residential street runs a deep, wide,
cemented ditch crossed by arching bridges, one to each house. These
great open conduits capture and channel the torrential rains, in their brief
but violent season, which otherwise would inundate every yard, home,
garage and sandbox and sweep them away through the gulleys of the
surrounding hills. A few beings tell stories of standing on the wood and
brick bridges during thunderous storms, when the whole sky is black
with water and sheets of water pour into the eyes; they tell of watching
tumbleweed, small trees, rabbits, porcupine, javelina, mule deer, even
once or thrice a small child, even once an adult male, being swept along
in the relentless flood, under one bridge and then another and another,
out of sight. And, in the case of this town, the swollen flood waters
would not be the color of water, but a profound blood-red, stained with
this land. The bodies along with all the flood debris were swept through
the cement ditches and through the huge drainage pipes on the outskirts
of the town, then down through gulleys into stony outwashes, where
they would be found, if they were found at all, bloated, unrecognizable,

scratched and bruised with rocks and branches, and the red fluid congealed all over them, perhaps still viscous, or dried crackling in the enormous sun.

There are two main streets, crossing each other at an intersection of silence. The business of such streets is simple. A barber shop, a small grocery, a post office, a small variety store, a corner drug store. Large spaces between, hardware, auto parts, unoccupied dirt lots, a café, a beauty parlor. Weedy lots, a church, a gas station a church. On the four corners of the main intersection, for which a stop sign is sufficient, are a gas station next to a fire station, a realtor and notary public, private residences, the funeral parlor. Always these places seem silent, empty, even when they are occupied. In short, the paraphernalia of any small town, with a pervasive mood of slow clocks, and fly-specked and faded display windows.

What is missing from these streets is a laundromat. There is a communal urge, followed strictly by each household, to wash all laundry in private. The history of such urges disappears backward in time, like this town's roads. No one would ever say precisely when or who; the law of secret washings is simply genetically known, and obeyed by all implicitly.

The sole café in town, also, next to the beauty salon, has white curtains drawn permanently in all windows and a realtor's sign taped inside the front window. The Red Inn, it was once called, after the color of the hills. Almost a gathering place in past days, almost lively, it too became at some point of indescribable time inappropriate. The owners changed the name briefly to Our Café, replacing red curtains, tablecloths and lampshades with creamy white décor. Then that name was removed also, the open sign in the window replaced with the realtor's sign, and the curtains drawn and the once bright red doors carefully recoated with white enamel closed in permanence.

Similarly, the town market, next to the post office, sells no fresh food. Almost no food at all. Rows of shelves are virtually bare; of food, that is. There are two short shelves in the rear of the store piled with five and ten pound white muslin sacks of various cereal grains, oats, corn, barley, millet, rice; and one long shelf along the side lined with cans of green vegetables, peas, beans, spinach, mustard greens, turnip greens, okra. Anything green, dark green, for those who crave some variety of color. But no fresh vegetables, no fresh fruits, of course no dairy or meat products. This mode of stocking the town's one grocery outlet was a more controversial decision than

the shutting of Our Café; it followed much debate waged between
those who still enjoyed soaking some oatmeal or wheatgerm in the
fluid, perhaps topped with fresh fruit (pale fruit, that is, like bananas;
never strawberries, never plums), versus those town members who
advocated a total self-sufficiency on the part of the entire town.

A compromise was reached, more in the service of compassion
than reason, as the supporters of self-reliance argued without
contradiction that all meat and iron-bearing vegetables were nutritiously
redundant. The bland and sugary boxed breakfast cereals and other
packaged dry foods were, no one disputed, no longer tasteable. As
for dairy products, fresh produce and the popular breads, all knew the
increasing difficulty, over time, in negotiating with even renegade,
unlicensed truckers from the outside to drive in fresh food supplies
daily. Even on a weekly basis; even semi-annually, as time went on,
as time does. Among town residents, no one needed to leave, to
venture out for any reason; no one needed to drive trucks back and
forth between the worlds, to supply the redundance of fresh food,
which was a waste of time, even in the guise of neighborliness. Here
you have a town satisfied with its hard-earned self-sufficiency, all
agreed, even the residents of weaker will.

But, to a perceived cruel deprivation of a continuing felt need,
the apotheosis of a lifetime's habits, in compromise, when presented
in those terms, agreement was reached with the ex-business partner
of one of the town's most successful citizens. From the large city 125
miles northward, transported by helicopter in shatter-proof bundles
to the virtually unused runway of the town airport (as potholed as
the town's roads), twice yearly from the sky in clear daylight
weather dropped the clean white sacks of cereal grains. Also the
small variety of canned vegetables. Something deep green, anything
green, for those who still existentially craved this one variety of
color. Spinach, okra.

What the market shelves did contain, items increasingly in
demand for some time, were disposable paper products. Paper
plates, paper napkins and tablecloths, rolls of paper towels. One
complete aisle on both sides held dozen-packs of paper clothing, the
square tissuey paper gowns with open backs and arm slits worn by
naked patients in doctors' examining rooms. These had been
obtained under certain conditions from a medical supply warehouse
across the border southward in a foreign country. Initially, all paper
products were trucked over this exotic international border and
deposited in the red rock and rattlesnake-infested southern outskirts

of the town. This, in sinister predawn hours of the imagination, among whispering and spitting negotiations in two languages of fair price, payoffs, risks and future orders.

The town council had felt demeaned by such negotiations, especially over paper products. Always they had defined themselves as bearers of civilization, while seeing their southern neighbors as genetic bandits. As it happened, the exchange of need and greed across this border had usually been in the other direction; but only the bandits held this view. The men of the town overwhelmingly preferred to deal with their own kind, but their own kind, still affecting official fear and/or horror, would not deal with them; yet. Need is need, as paper is paper. Twice monthly, with the town fund established for this purpose, five rotating volunteers bought on the 3 a.m. deserted border dozens of large cases of paper towels and napkins and tablecloths from the foreigners. Never did they notice that the foreigners were also embarrassed by this scenario, trained as they were to deal in the more manly contraband, drugs and submachineguns; nor that the bitterly large bundles of green paper given the foreign bandits in trade for all the white paper were, in the bandits' minds, a fair exchange for what they perceived as risking their necks in the presence of vampires.

Strange, a town thought never to change, or to change too slowly for verification. Women with lives invested in hierarchies of china, who set out elaborate Sunday dinnertables of gold-rimmed china and heirloom embroidered linen napkins on linen tablecloths, whether guests were dining or not; even for the silent eating of two people. Women who could not dream of using paperplates even in the backyard in summer, because they were flimsy and lazy, and men who would not dream of eating from them, who could in the recent past easily hurl them against the wall, piled full of food, and demand respect. Three sets of dinnerware per household, this was the standard: the painted gold-rim china for holidays and guests, the plain gold-rim for Sunday afternoon dinners, very good stoneware for weekday and Saturday meals. Women whose households could not afford to meet this standard could at least uphold the ideal by envying it, and seeking good imitations.

This was a way of life. It did not change abruptly. But, staining the lovely cups, saucers, plates, gravy bowls, china ladles; then, washing those stained dishes in the same stain, whether in the raw hemorrhage of the kitchen sink, or in the surgical racks of the automatic dishwasher which were hidden away, but there. The truth was, it would not wash off; something red and sticky always remained on the spoons, terrible rusty stains spread over the table linen. Beginning with paper plates, then paper napkins, paper tablecloths, the beings of the town did not succumb to any personal self-indulgence or modern trend; they succumbed to their own character which, whether public or private, was rational. Rational beings could see clearly that disposable paper eating products were the only rational solution; no room for nostalgia.

Beginning with paper plates, then, the town gradually but eventually changed over many of its proud daily habits in the name of practicality. But not strange, such changes, fundamentally. They were deep in this town's unchanging tradition of recognizing necessity, and being up to it. The transition from china and linen to paper plates and paper napkins was a sane response to a central felt need of the entire community, for disposability. It was not custom they wanted to dispose of, all knew, but a problem that could not be disposed of customarily. The evolution to paper plates truly maintained the town's tradition of remaining the same while adapting, with no tears. When a few households after visits to the abandoned local hospital appeared at their dinner tables wearing the tissuey examination gowns, retrieved as a stroke of ingenuity from the medical supply cupboards that had been left, very quickly, and almost full, no one raised an eyebrow. These paper examination gowns would never replace streetwear or household clothing; they were short, thin and immodest. But as a kind of all-over white bib worn at the dining table, they were sanitary and helpful. With arrangements made, under certain conditions, with the medical supply warehouse over the southern border, the paper gowns became an item of daily use in the town. They were obtained, without much risk, just over the border in stipulated darkness via an exchange of large semi-sterilized plastic transfusion bottles, much in need in the foreign country, and quite full.

Thus, for once, need met need in the continuous bookkeeping of the night.

On one old habit, however, every household in town agreed: all refused to concede to plastic eating utensils, plastic forks, plastic spoons, plastic knives. In no way. On every kitchen and diningroom table in every home the traditional family silver continued to be laid out. In some cases, the floral pattern for holidays, Sundays and guests, and the plain pattern for daily use. The silverware, unlike the dishware and linen, could be rubbed clean with good silverpolish; it was extra work, but worth it. The lingering tang of iron was incidental. Actually, only spoons were really used, dinner and soup spoons and silver labels; but the full silver setting was laid out, proudly, with each meal. It was a way of honoring one's history in the ongoing floodtide of events; and plastic spoons were impossible.

The toilets, also; the bathroom sinks. The automatic washing machine on the back porch. They all took some adjustment, some time. As the president of the town council remarked in private, no one ever said life was easy. There was always that gush of red fluid in the bathroom sink, that fountain of red in the once immaculate white toilet bowl. And of course the red streak on the toilet paper. The men of the town, and the many post-menopausal women, needed a serious period of adjustment to the new fact that they were forever going to appear, in the bathroom, to be having menstrual periods. But they did adjust; in all the bathrooms, in silence, in privacy, where such things have always been adjusted.

As for the washing machines, the whole problem of clothing and laundry, it was quickly found by each woman that every material, no matter what color, when washed in a mixture of 2/3 fluid with 1/3 dry bleach, two spin rinses (cold water wash), emerged a kind of irregular greenish tan, reminiscent of camouflaged combat uniforms. This seemed spartan at first, but became normal.

Normal, in fact, is what everything becomes, when beings strive simply to make it so. Some world news reports about this town, when it first became known, described its residents as "amazing." Not so. Not amazing at all, how each being adjusted in private, in personal silence, without benefit of public discussion or state instruction, or liberal psychotherapy or college extension courses. These beings, of this town, were of solid stock, with generations stretching behind them, with a history and long habit of practicing the rational art of private, silent adjustment to Anything.

So, this was the life of this town, the daily life of its beings. And what of the source of this life? What of the source of any life.

One road leading from town, unlike the other roads seemingly going nowhere, heads northwest for 2 ¼ miles through rolling hills to the Excavation Site. This stretch of two-lane road through arterially red hills is devoid of vegetation; one could say the large, sticky clumps strewn around the land's surface were a typical flora of such hills, if flora was understood almost poetically. Under torrential rains, these huge clots break up, dissolve, incarnadine the floodwaters pouring through the gulleys; in storm winds they shake and quiver; under the sun, they shine, congeal on the surface, crack open as scabs on wounds to reveal the viscous pulsing within. As some dissolve, others appear; indeed as flowers, or clots in veins, something organically growing. Apart from these, no brush or cacti, no dark or even pale green thing. The thin gray road moves up and down through hills of blood, that is all.

An unbearably monotonous landscape, that is, were it never to end. But it does. A slow curve around one large hill brings the road to its destination. There, suddenly, signs of enterprise: a corrugated aluminum shack, two parked trucks, lengths of rusted pipe and long rot-eaten timbers stacked in measured heaps against a chain-link fence. And this fence, stretching out in both directions in an enormous circle, a metalloid embrace, surround the vast hole of the Excavation Site; the Pit, as it is called by local dwellers. One must park the car and walk to the fence, look through it, to view the hole's extent and depth. And color; the almost indescribable color and texture of the insides of the Pit.

From the top rim downward, sheer cascades of colors: mauve, gold, rust, purple, pink, silver, blue, incandescent turquoise. Streaks of orange, streaks of fire, yellow streaks of toxic arsenic. Radioactive greens of lime and fungus. Each color spilled over the others, in corroded terraced levels, channeled by erosion, avalanched by rain, crusted, broken open, merged; each geologic texture, as though alive, crawling over the variegated lumps and rubble of the earthly flesh that came before. And over this, the solid spills of individual rocks, orthorhombic crystals, dredging gears, rusted-out elbows, coils of wire, buttons, nails, hair curlers, stray lead bullets, all runneling, flowing in geological slow motion one over another down to the center of the hole. Deep, deep down. The entire technological history of the Pit was thus laid bare to any observer, in concentric layer after layer, vast polychronic slide upon slide, sloping down from the first simple surface diggings, by hand and stick, of the precivilized beings, immemorial years ago, downward through sediments of beauty, sediments of grief, sediments of nothing very important or useful, sediments of historical overthrow, one solid layer of crushed bones; and then further down the notable sediments of great wealth and petrochemical power, sediments of capital gains, sediments of wrapping paper, one solid sedimentary level each of glass, electrical conducting alloy, and stockpiled war materiel.

As the Pit funneled to its center, narrowing, deep, full sunlight only briefly touched those levels and they remained to most viewers a mosaic of bluish shadow; a metal sign attached to the chain-link fence diagrammed these most-recently uncovered sediments and listed their mined contents. Some of which were quite famous. But then the raw earth funnel stopped, became a pool of liquid. A pool of dense, oblique color, sometimes dark red, brown, almost black, it changed with the movement of shadows; or, in the glare of a full sun directly overhead, it blazed thick fiery red, and then like a mirror threw back light. That was all. It was very difficult to get a cool, unshadowed, unglazed view of the actual blood-red color and viscosity of the fluid, and the aerial photographers who attempted flyovers of the pit's pool in search of popular postcard shots had all been disappointed in their attempts. Most had settled for afternoon slants which were romantic, but murky.

The color of this pool had changed with the uncovering and mining of each successive level; with sulfur, long ago, it was yellow, and earlier with azurite it was radiant blue, and of course much shallower. The pool's fluid had been all possible geologic colors, and from some levels intense or muddy mixtures of colors. When, from the previously saturated black ore sediments, printer's ink was extracted, the pool had become an icon of Total Ink; an utter, hard-edged blackness that seemed no pool at all, no thing but a gaping hole into an underworld, where Nothingness was buried. But then that strata also was sponged and suctioned out, piped clean of its ink, and the present color had flooded in. Or, in reality's slow motion, the pool had been pure ink, then ink admixtured with blood, then almost all blood, then pure blood; an organic-technological process. Some people claimed they could smell it, the ink, the blood, that is, and the change from one to the other; but this claim was open to dispute. Such things are hard to distinguish, at deep levels; the Pit is wide, the pool is very far down. One things only is known, that almost continuously small rocks, bullets, ball bearings, curlers, solid strewn crystals, etc., are dislodging, eroding, meandering, rolling, rolling down the ruined terraced slopes into the ambiguous pool at the center, to disappear in its deep well. This has been going on for decades. But the pool continues unblocked, unplugged; nothing fills it up. It is apparently "bottomless," that is, deeper than all past imagination.

No living person knows when the open pit digging began. At one time a thriving Mine Museum was located on the two-lane road, among rolling hills (then simply coarse red dirt splotched with green bushes), halfway between town and the Excavation Site. Lively small-scale models of the various mining methods used throughout the years were on display, and glass cases containing historic mining tools, unusual safety equipment, ore samples and examples of all the other products that had been dug out; charts and diagrams on the walls showed where each mined object came from, along the levels of the Pit, and where it went, into the world, after appropriate processing, packaging, marketing. Historic display cases dramatized the first civilized beings arriving in the region, in wagons and on horseback; they found the indigenous naked creatures squatting in the dirt, digging up small geological objects with bare hands and pointed sticks. Thus the Pit's origin, in what was then only a slight depression of the earth, a sandy little dip. The objects sought by the natives were simple gem stones, turquoise, azurite, malachite, roughly polished and used ornamentally. In the childlike mental grasp of these early beings there was no concept of serious mining, a factor which helped account for their elimination.

With settlement, mining began in earnest at the present site. Men came from everywhere, attracted by the adventure. As several posters in the Mine Museum put it, the town grew with the expansion of "the Pit," and the Pit grew as an expression of the town's spirit. It grew, as all know, into the largest intentional hole on the earth's surface. Innovators, in the early years, introduced various subterranean approaches to the extraction of ores from the earth, but the straightforward digging of a hole, deeper and deeper into the ground, always seemed the most expeditious method for this terrain. Several hundred males, equipped with picks and shovels, simply began digging; as the hole grew, timbers were used to shore up the higher levels of dirt, and these shorings congealed into a circumference of terraces. Later, tracks were built, for rail cars, and mules brought in to haul them; deeper down, around and around; the workforce grew from a few hundred to thousands. When ground water seeped into the working levels, as it did more often at greater depths, giant sponges were brought in to soak up the intruding fluids. When water flooded in, violently,

without warning, drowning hundreds of workers, and burying
hundreds more beneath tons of collapsed earth, the sponges were
hooked up behind the mule-drawn rail cars and dragged down and
around the wet circumference, gradually soaking up the waters.
The sponges were periodically wrung out by giant rollers (similar
to old-fashioned washing machine wringers), into the rail cars,
and the water hauled by more patient mules around and upward to
the dry surface; the method was a simple as it was efficient. Drowned
bodies were usually soaked up also, lodging in the sponge holes,
and removed by the same process; if not, the bones were extracted
by shovels from dried sediments at a later date. At great depths,
the sponges were working constantly, and pipe systems were eventually
installed to transport the fluids, which at some point became
quite valuable.

The first substances mined were ordinary gold and silver.
These were found in veins of upthrust quartz, just below the surface,
where the naked creatures had scratched and clawed their savage
jewelry from loose dirt. Soon, large globs of copper appeared, and
as the gold and silver deposits dwindled, the copper became
abundant; by the turn of the century, this Pit was known as the
world's largest, most lucrative copper mine, a model of productivity.
Death tolls for workers drowned, crushed or suffocated ranged
between 1,582 and 1,826 (the discrepancy involved accurate bone-
counting), but fortunes made by the legendary few during this
period were specific tallies of personal enterprise. (A glass case
in the Museum contained mementos of the Copper Boom: silk
top hats, gold and ruby or emerald lorgnettes and imported Chinese
fans worn by the mine owners and their spouses to the Opera
House, located in a fabulous city 850 miles to the northwest.
Facsimiles of steamer tickets, also, representing their many
romantic ocean voyages. A diamond-studded dog collar worn by
one of their poodles when taken out by a chauffeur for short
walks along the fabulous boardwalk of a renounced city 2,050
miles to the northeast. And so forth.) It was an extraordinary
time. The town's main street was developed, with board sidewalks,
several taverns, two hotels that served as brothels, assay office,
mercantile store, even a branch bank; mine foremen built
respectable two-story houses all in a row. Apart from the local
railcar line transporting dirt from the mine to the tailings pile, a
small freight railway connected the town with a large city 200
miles eastward; loose shacks inhabited by workers clustered

along this track, and those who did not drown, become crushed or
suffocate frequently got drunk. The copper lasted about 24 ½
years.

When it ran out, the town waited in a hopefully apprehensive
mood for the appearance of the next native element. Geologists
hired to fabricate evidence of diamond pipes at a subsequent depth
predicted, with the nodding mine owners, that this announcement
would provoke a good two weeks of mass voluntary digging.
Two weeks passed, three weeks, with shovels flying and several
tragic cave-ins; four weeks, five weeks. Workers were digging
up nothing but dirt, and each other's bones. Stocks plummeted,
one brothel and the branch bank closed, and the mine owners
could not be reached for comment as the once vast working force
of thousands dwindled to a skeleton crew of 123. After nine weeks
of unproductive, unpaid loyal digging, 22 miners remained in a
town that had become a ghost town, brothelless, with tumbleweed
and loose dust from a very large hole blowing down the otherwise
unoccupied main street.

In later days those 22 shovellers would be spoken of with awe.
Haggard, half-naked, hollow-eyed, they spaced themselves out
around this Pit's internal circumference, sometimes knee-deep in
mud and odious femurs, and continued digging. Mining was all they
knew. They could not believe this great hole had yielded up its
final wealth. Sun, rain and dirt pelted them, several shovels fractured
and rotted in their hands, so often the whole sky disappeared
from their view and the difference between day and night became
rudimentary. By now 1,095 feet down in the Pit, they grappled
with the literal bowels of the earth. No one counted time, so it
became eternal. As beings already condemned to the depths of Hell,
unwashed automatons glued to their shovels with gruesome
blisters of flesh, so far down they were mere specks forever, they
had but one thought: they were on to something. In later estimates
they dug for five months and 26 days. And then it struck.

One shovel, then another, then another, all became simultaneously entangled in a sediment of rotting cloth. Throwing the
shovels aside, dropping to their knees, they dug and clawed like
maniacs with trembling fingers. Out came three solid feet of
compressed oily rags, old underwear, dead uniforms, ripped sheets
and filthy things like bloody gauze bandages and monogrammed
used handkerchiefs. These items were utterly disgusting and
useless; yet the 20 crazed miners (two had disappeared) tossed

the pussy bandages and foul drawers into the air like holy confetti, moaned, wept, pressed the dung and disease-encrusted uniforms, etc., to their parched lips and kissed, deeply, like icons. Unpleasant, yes; but where such nasty garbage exists, true wealth is not far behind.

All pain and weariness gone, they gathered up the stinking mess into a huge heap to be disposed of later, and continued digging. They dug carefully now, watchfully, often with bare hands, scanning monotonous dirt for any sign of a change in texture, or color. After eight hours the earth became moist, more like oily than watery, and darkened from mud brown to a slick, blackish gray. They dug. No sound of speech was necessary, they had all stopped speaking long ago. One mind told them they were close to something; they dug throughout a pitchy, moonless night into the dawn. As light trickled slowly over the Pit's horizon, far above, one digger straightened up, sighed, and pushed his shovel heavily into the dirt. The sound returned was not the dull sigh of earth, but a clink of metal.

In a cold sweat, on his knees, he cleared away the oily mud with both hands. With one delicate forefinger he created a dark little hole in the dark oily earth. One moment, two moments; the eternal pause of great moments. Then out it poured: a pure stream of gears. The flow of gears was steady, shining, perfect; as the earth loosened, larger gears poured out. The flow thickened, piled up, cascaded; four of the miners were drowned, crushed, suffocated by gears before they could clamber to higher levels of the Pit, escaping on frantic hands and knees.

And thus the great mine was restored to life, and economic productivity. Twenty-two brave if crazed beings had wrestled with the earth's entrails, and emerged (16 of them) covered with glory. Through their berserk labor, the terrestrial innards had revealed, not raw nothingness, but signs of profound civilization. The mine owners, some with changed names, returned from the edge of bankruptcy, announcing that the hole was more than a mine, it was henceforth to be known as a Gear Industry. They took over, as before, the profitable management of everything. Of the 22 original heroic shovellers who had singlemindedly contributed to the acquisition of this great new wealth, thirteen who hadn't been drowned, suffocated or crushed were committed to mental institutions, while three were promoted to foremen. Rapidly they built three two-story respectable houses, all in a row, with inter-

esting statuary in their front yards, composed of large cement
replicas of gears.

And thus the resurrection of the town. This time it was
repopulated without brothels, a solid family town, appealing not
to wild, irregular bachelor miners but to steady, hopelessly
entrenched moral beings. The type of beings from whom, hence-
forward, the town's peculiar character and style were to grow.
Not glamorous as gold, silver or copper, the gear was infinitely
more necessary; and the more gears poured from the Pit, the more
were necessary uses invented for them. Highways, automobiles
and weapons factories, airplanes and wars were mysteriously
breaking out all over the globe; these industries demanded gears,
as gears demanded them. It was with gear production that the
town's first real money was made, not exported entirely to an
absentee owner class, but put in the bank accounts of town residents
themselves; those smart few beings, that is, of the new middle
-management echelon who were simply clever enough to devise
cheap, efficient methods of boxing and distributing gears to all
corners of the earth now clamoring for gears. Government
contracts poured in also; the town prospered patriotically. In
addition to the post office flag, which was mandatory, the Town
Council appropriated money to erect two very tall flagpoles at
both ends of the main street, coming and going. The proudest
flag flew, of course, at the entrance to the Gear Pit; and, because
some of the new boxing methods did require workers to risk
being drowned, crushed or suffocated by the outpouring of gears
as, e.g., they crouched on moving assembly belts holding open
large cartons while slowly circling 2 ½ feet below the Pit's lower
circumference of newly dug horizontal holes in the oily embankments
trying to effectively capture the thundering fresh streams of gears
flowing from the earth at precisely 1,598 gears a minute (755 to
a box), there was also a bronze plaque embedded in cement at the
base of the pit's flagpole commemorating all those who gave
their lives unthinkingly in the production of gears for the
National Defense.

(One Mine Museum wall had been filled with charts, graphs
and photos describing the critical historic role played by the
production of billions and billions of gears in the development of
20th century mass warfare; and it was considerable. But the gear
had its pacific, whimsical and even attractive uses. A glass case
displayed gear ashtrays, gear paperweights, a lamp base made

entirely of gears; a complete jewelry set of gear signet ring, gear tie-clasp, gear cufflinks and gear belt buckle for males, with a companion set, for the ladies, of gear earrings, brooch, bracelet and necklace. Most impressive was a two-foot high completely gear-constructed dove of peace, carrying in its beak in lieu of olive branch a twist of silver-alloy wire with flowery clusters of assorted gears dangling from either end. All these items were designed, constructed and welded by ordinary Pit workers entirely at their own expense and on their own time; a real show of spirit.)

When the gears ran out, no problem. The legendary gear was followed in quick succession by equally enormous outpourings of nails, ballbearings, screws, the aforementioned lead bullets, and office paper clips. Car windshields and batteries alternated with hand grenades and gas masks. At one point cigarette lighters flowed out at the rate of 1,523 per minute in precise alternation with 1,523 cans of lighter fluid; this was troublesome when they ignited each other (due to worker error) and the entire level erupted in a blazing inferno of metallic flames reaching almost to the Pit's rim. It burned for three nights and three days. Untold numbers of workers were lost, along with the tragic destruction of 8,632,948 cans of lighter fluid and 8,632,948 cigarette lighters.

When the smoke cleared, the pit revealed walls of char and molten rivulets; a season's rain was needed to wash down the blackness. A pool of thick, sooty fluid accumulated at the Pit's center, an uneasy, unspongeable pool. A pool that did not sink back into the soil through absorption, or weariness, but had seemingly begun to well up from this deep pore of earth like black sweat, or serum in a wound. This was a difficult time. The fire had sealed over, cauterized the hundreds of thousands of productive little holes from which such great abundance had recently poured. The earth was streaked with hardness, a surface meld of alloys from so many stray bullets, gears, paper clips, cigarette lighters, etc. Newly recruited workteams went down into the Pit to dig, not with delicate forefingers, but with pickaxes and sledgehammers. As they shattered, uprooted, peeled back this fused metalloid carapace from large scarred flanks and thighs of the damaged inner hole, they uncovered raw blotches of more disgusting things: layers upon layers of half-corroded used sanitary napkins, douche bags, enema hoses and syringes, broken, rotten teeth, and the overwhelming stench of something dead. As before, but with increased efficiency, these nauseating items were gathered into

large heaps and disposed of immediately. (The death smell of
course lingered until the production of aerosol cans.) And then
around the edges of these picked scabs, as it were, from around
the nocturnal fringes of such terrible scars and unmentionable
uses, something new began to ooze. A gooey substance, pellucid
green in color. Shyly at first, and then with increasing ebullience,
it crept and flowed and jiggled over the lower Pit surface,
covering over the recent devastation like an innocent vegetation
or spring grass. Something about it invited tasting. Several workers
vomited at the thought. But then one, then another, then another
and another, bent over and dipped a delicate forefinger in the
happy green substance overwhelming their rubber boots, now,
to the knees; and tasted. And found it good.

Lime gelatin.

It was mid-century. A difficult period had been experienced,
But a challenging one. As before, so now, sheer persistence had
won through. The same caliber of beings willing to dig through
sediments of crusty bandages and foul snot rags in the pursuit
of gears, had now managed to pick and wade through sex and a
half feet of bloody Qotex and other abominations to reach a
pure and lucid exudation of green Gello. Of that tough crew of 94,
the fast-moving three who were not drowned and suffocated by
it (hardly crushed) were given bonuses. A new era had begun.
First the lime gelatin was bottled, then sold in tubes like toothpaste;
the outside consultant bred to design a method of drying the
gelatin into powder before packaging it was, with great success,
promoted to vice-president, and a clause was inserted in the new
pension plan to help cover certain medical expenses incurred by
those workers who might suffer long-term side effects from the
extensive radiation they were exposed to during the drying process.
The Mine Museum exhibited, not the gelatin dessert itself of course,
but two shelves of aluminum molds used by local females in
making their renowned Lime Gelatin Supreme. Moods were
lifted by the green Gello, and as it oozed steadily from the Pit's
steep funnel onto giant cookie sheets held up by teams of gloved
and goggled workers for 43 ½ seconds each under huge ultraviolet
lamps suspended from enormous booms swung out over the Pit's
vast rim, experts stationed in radiation-proof booths watched
carefully for signs of an expected change in the gelatin's color,
from lime green to strawberry perhaps, or orange or raspberry.
This change never came.

Instead, with no warning, at 9:05 on a Monday morning, the hole erupted like a fountain. A department store fountain. From six higher levels of formerly fire-sealed holes, around the entire circumference, hundred of thousands of gallons per minute began to pour in hundreds of thousands of vari-colored streams, for the first time in the Pit's history not successively but simultaneously: red, orange and pink nail polish, pastel hair curlers, wax and varnish remover, 50 shades of shampoo-in hair color, facial creams, and thirteen different exotic perfumes. An incredible sight, a circular niagara of arcing, roaring, multicolored assorted urinations, each mezzanine-like level spouting tens of thousands of streams cascading down through each level of tens of thousands of streams vigorously spouting below; all drilling, roiling, spuming into the frothy pool of lime gelatin heaving and quivering at the bottom. A moment before, the pit had swarmed with 3,587 goggled Gello-driers, fresh from a weekend of rest and relaxation; those few left alive, 45 management personnel observing from the top of the Pit, stood in awe. These were female commodities spouting, like water from a sieve, or blood from a mass execution. A shift to the distaff side had definitely occurred with the appearance of lime gelatin; on the spot, the hole's name was officially changed to The Mercantile Pit, and a whole new approach to feminized packaging and world distribution discussed and diagrammed. The Mine Museum, for the first time in its history, hired two local female beings as guards; one answered cosmetics questions in relation to the glass case exhibits of, e.g., 50 different shades of wash-in shampoo, and the other guided female visitors to the new toilet facility that had just been constructed 60 yards east of the museum for their convenience. There was some debate about removing the gelatin molds from their museum shelves, since despite great filtering efforts management had decided the lime Gello was no longer a profitable item, "due to production problems," as they stated to the press; after three and a half hours of closed-door discussion, the aluminum molds were reclassified as "of minor historical value" and removed to a high, dusty shelf in the rear of the Museum. Following two unsuccessful attempts to separate out thousands of pairs of goggles and plastic gloves from the gelatinous stew (no longer green in color), the deeply contaminated lime Gello was simply siphoned off, dried, pulverized, and sold under a different brand name as "mixed fruit cocktail delight" in the foreign country across the southern border.

barbara mor

And what of the town? A long, luminous mesa comprised
its northwestern horizon. A mesa composed of mine tailings,
carried by rail from the Excavation Site, heaped levels, lumps and
streaks of orange, purple and blue-green superfused with flashes of
metal and splintered glass. This mesa glowed uncannily in moonlight,
even more so on moonless nights, and no tree or bush grew on it.
Up against this magnificent backdrop, as in affirmation of the
source of wealth, the homes of the town's richest citizens were built.
Five fine two-story mansions with surrounding brick walls and
wrought-iron gates on which bronze plaques were affixed saying
Beggars and Peddlers Not Welcome.

Descending from this arcanum, block after block of more
humble one and two-story abodes, all in a row. Low stone walls,
hedges, picket fences, dry little gardens, and very unique lawn décor
composed of large-scale cement replicas of paper clips, nail polish
bottles, and six-inch mortar shells. Several of the town's long-term
citizens had increased their bank accounts by inventing real
estate. Straggling along the railroad tracks, block after block of
abandoned, collapsing miners' shacks occupying narrow lots were
bought up for virtually nothing; refurbished with bright paint, with
added garages and back porches, these tiny houses were rented
out to ordinary workers in return for very large portions of their
wages.

All prospered. Periodically, toxic fumes released by the
mine's more exotic products required sudden evacuations of the
whole town, followed by mass burials of those failing to run fast
enough. At the Excavation Site itself, there were the usual cave-ins,
spontaneous explosions, fires, failures of fluid-sponging procedures
and so forth, leaving hundreds of workers crippled, amputated,
blinded, gassed, charred, drowned, crushed, suffocated or
mysteriously missing, with resultant devastation of families. Through
it all, the town's honest citizens remained intact and forward-
thinking; the unfortunate disappeared; and the rich throve. On the
main streets, three more branch banks were instituted, and the
daily newspaper gained a reputation for reporting only good news;
in its rare absence, columns were filled with historical sketches
and local recipes.

When, after more than two decades of reliable production,
the town was confronted with the sudden cessation of feminine

cosmetic products and furniture wax, a front-page banner headline read simply "New Era Dawns?", followed by six pages of birth, death and wedding announcements, thick-bordered church invitations, and quickly-collected recipes for every type of dessert on earth except gelatin. The men who entered the Pit, masked, rubber-coated and cautious, reported a corresponding black border around each rock, crystalline lump, stray bullet, lipstick tube and aerosal spray can within their purview. Halfway down the terraced slope they experienced an intense blackness seeping from cracks and erosions, welling mutely around their boots; and the pool at the center was no longer nacreous or tessellated by the ambitious mixture of so many oily, astringent and plastoid things. It was pure Ink.

   True blackness. As it were, the serum of such news, as white flesh is its paper. A convention of editors meeting synchronously in a large city 225 miles to the northwest was flown in to verify the fluid; after nineteen minutes of deliberation they climbed from the Pit in single file, each with a solid black border around his body, as a residue or solemn halo. They spoke of the unmeasureable contribution of printer's ink to the civilized economy and world political order, to the business of journalism and literary publication not to mention the cartoon industry. Television and newsphoto cameras flashed, capturing the ink aura surrounding these beings; meanwhile the Town Council initiated emergency mop-up operations to deal with the terrific, widening black stain that had begun perhaps as a leak in the Pit's pipes but was now spreading, down the arroyos, into the town's gutters, up through cracks in streets, sidewalks and dusty lawns, seeping, flowing and splotching with the seasons' first hard rains as a kind of journalistic hemorrhage.

   Hundreds of thousands of unused perfume bottles were relabeled, filled with black fluid. The increased use of ink in daily life was definitively studied and encouraged. Informational tours into and out of the Pit were conducted for all the world's journalism students and newspaper reporters; as they emerged, outlined in black, they were handed complimentary bottles of ink along with a pamphlet authorized by the town's editor-in-chief extolling the patriotic uses of good news. Plans were underway for a Mine Museum exhibit and symposium documenting the fascinating correlation between news accounts of reality and the absolute non-existence of that reality, when the first hesitant reports began coming in to the effect that the ink was turning red.

In sub rosa, predawn hours mine managers armed with fountain pens entered the Pit. Over a period of several days top-secret codes moved back and forth between the town and centers of government and world trade. There was some mention of a quick promotional campaign advocating the "natural earth tones" of brownish-reddish ink. But by now the pool at the Pit's center was clearly viscid red; when the managers went to test it, their pens clogged, or the words they wrote all looked like death scrawls. And the air was saturated with a thick odor, unlike all others; Dobermans guarding the town's five mansions howled day and night, an incessant whining that became invisible, inaudible as the voice of everything and everyone.

It soaked the rolling hills, pushing gelatinous clots to the surface of coarse dirt. Cracks in the sidewalks filled with red, cement and dust lots permeated with red stains. Red flowing gutters, the flood ditches awash with red. Citizens sprayed driveways and garages with lawn hoses, trying to prevent the disfigurement of cars. But the blood seeped everywhere, and the arroyos surrounding the town were as open veins. The tailings pile began, as it were, to bleed. The five large mansions at its foot, of gray stucco and yellow brick, were perennially streaked and stained with erosions of arsenic, green gelatin, nail polish, or most recently bizarre calligraphies of black ink. Now the mess turned fully sanguine, scarlet rivulets and clots oozed, melted, loosened, flowed down in the rain and heat, and the cultivated gardens were strewn with sticky bright clumps and massive blood puddles. Trees and bushes began to suck up the red fluid from their roots, as did the porous walls of the great houses. Within five days it had entered the town's water supply. A mine manager, sprinkling his front lawn in the summer evening of a dry day, turned his hose on a little garden patch of cacti, oleander and budding agave. The black-flecked water spraying out suddenly turned to rust, clogged, and then with explosive force began pouring a stream of pure blood. With the mental control of an executive he continued spraying plants, a perfect, silent adjustment to this final change, as the red viscosity covered his lawn and garden, his gray pants and canvas shoes, with spatters, globs and blotches of an irrepressible bloody dew.

For his nextdoor neighbor, the event marked the beginning of a fascinating hobby: a study of the growth effects of spilled blood on local desert vegetation. He recorded the quick disappearance of all known varieties of flowers, and gave his name to a pale green sword-like plant springing up everywhere from the dead flora. Most of all, he declared the problem of chlorosis, or yellow-leaf plant anemia, had with this new diet disappeared from the town forever.

Doctors and nurses also disappeared; with the appearance of blood in the water pipes, the entire small hospital staff fled, citing a conflict of interest. With great regret, the Town Council was forced to close the Mine Museum. The few visitors who did come, after the news got out, were reluctant to park their cars and then walk 25 yards through sticky, scarlet clots to the Museum entrance. In high winds the clots moved, like tumbleweeds of blood. A bridge was built, to accommodate these tourists; but the gluey blobs continued to mass and ooze on the threshold and pile up against the Museum windows. Beings not used to it found this offensive. With the cessation of the tourist trade, the town's residents also realized the market shelves had grown quite bare; no food had been delivered for weeks. At this point the Town Council voted to become officially self-sufficient. Indeed, with blood flowing freely through all the town's plumbing, from home faucets, from drinking fountains in banks and gas stations and even the dusty park, most beings had become quite satisfied with this diet. They had simply, without fuss, grown used to it. And for those who still craved grains and green beans, those accommodations were made.

Some worried about the town's isolation. Incoming roads were silent, mail to and from the outside world ceased. Rarely, a small private airplane flew over in late afternoon, attempting colored postcard shots of the Pit; but these were sensationalists, who never landed, who were not interested in the ordinary, daily life of the town. In a lonely show of spirit, the postmaster and two postal workers devised a combination stamp and postmark for the local mail. Using sponges soaked in blood from the bathroom tap, they dipped and affixed their bloody thumbprints to the top righthand corner of every envelope dropped through their slots. Unfortunately, town residents had little to say to each other, by mail or otherwise; the post office closed. Eventually the postal workers were reemployed as trash burners at the dumpsite east of town. They now shovel great white and red heaps of paper products into the flames, blood-saturated napkins, tablecloths and medical gowns that smoulder and crackle thickly throughout the night, releasing a stench similar to burning corpse flesh; which, of course, everyone has grown used to.

As for a larger world, its expressions of horror, shock, outrage, etc., since the blood was first struck, five years ago, a well of gore seemingly with no cease or bottom; it was predictable. Town residents recalled similar reactions to the first unearthing of gears; even more so to the dramatic eruptions of perfume and plastic hair curlers. Rational memory tells them that in time all had come around; as, in time, all does. Emissaries from the barbaric nations, habitually torn by hunger and war, would in time arrive at the town's southern border clandestinely to negotiate for large, full transfusion bottles. Civilized governments such as their own would dispatch teams of well-armed technical engineers to gather further information on the region's geology; they would want to know how similar subterranean bloodpits could be uncovered, or indeed constructed, in other parts of the globe. For several unimaginable uses. It might take ten years, more or less, for worldly recognition; the town was equipped to wait. (Meanwhile, one shy but reliable signal of a return to the ordinary had already occurred. International agents from the world's largest paper products manufacturing corporation, approaching Town Council members via aliases after midnight on the privacy of the southern border, had tentatively offered one year's free supply of paper napkins, tablecloths, towels, toilet tissue rolls and medical gowns in exchange for the town's exclusive endorsement. This arrangement fell through only because the paper company was adamantly promoting a line of modern, color-coordinated deep pastel pinks, aquas, lilacs and orange-rust shades upon which clots and bloodstains looked more than necessarily garish.

But, the breakthrough occurred. The town awaits an offer of white products.)

From its experience, the town has learned something profound about the nature of its own will, as of the mysterious hidden resources of the Earth. Deeper and deeper, as it had descended into the dark downward and abysm not solely of time but of its own evolution, what it had dug with its historic fingers from this soiled Hole, so to speak, was an implacable knowledge others could profit from, if others would: That the inexorable becomes the simply inextricable, and thus the normal; and vice versa. If only beings strive to make it so. The question of whose blood is never raised. Nor, if the hole extends through the globe to China, could it be Communist blood? Intellectual quibbling is extraneous to the town's experience of itself.

Some beings from the outside have called the pit a Living Wound, citing the bloodflow as a strong proof. But morbid and negative metaphors do not make the world turn; as gears do, for example, or ball bearings. Or as now, the mining of blood.

Beings are very pale here, as befits their genetic heritage. In other places, they will point out – Africa, Asia, Latin America – people have good color. But they die like flies. Here, though pale and elderly, the lifespan seems to be lengthening. On a diet of pure blood, no one is immortal, but also no one has died. One household became very ill but that was attributed to an overindulgence of canned spinach, which is toxic.

The predictably few visitors to the town must of course eat the local fare. Any tourists trying surreptitiously to gather up the limited cans of dark green vegetables is given bad looks; the grocery clerk spurns their money and returns the cans to the shelves. The town feels it has no place for types who come to gawk, or Write magazine articles; anyone who sincerely wants to know this town, they argue, must eat what this town eats. And then make comments, or be silent.

As this town is not strange, but silent.

A metabolic silence. Reptiles on rocks in sunlight, the flat red angles of heat surrounding them. Or the empty roads lolling towards town in silent thirst, like long black tongues among the red hills. Or, sitting on front porches in the evening cool, following a violent thunderstorm, as the sky and trees are washed and clear of dust accumulation, listening to silence and the river of blood rushing through the deep cement drainage veins along one side of the street; under the bridges, through the town's sticky gutters and sewage pipes into the burning red arroyos. Or, sponging up the remains of a small backyard dinner, a Sunday picnic among friends; the patio spattered with familiar red spots, the scarlet ice cubes all melted in the paper cups. Taking a bath or shower; spraying cacti with the lawn hose; cleaning the splotched car daily with smuggled jars of silverware polish and several large scouring pads. Or, simply, just standing at the kitchen sink, taking a long refreshing drink from the family faucet.

A metabolism of silent satisfaction, that is, for the simple, earned pleasures of life. Those who run from it deny a personal and private, yet common adjustment, that could be shared by all.

Behind the town, the bloody mesa of mine tailings glows fixedly in darkness. In daylight, it seeps and pulsates, seemingly a living thing, streaked with thousands of rivulets of red fluid clogged with shining thrombi. Beyond it, the Pit, with its bottomless well of blood. Staunchless, silent blood, i.e., which seems to be always flowing, visibly and subterraneanly, towards all horizons. As the town consumes the blood, silently, and silently recycles it, returning towards these horizons its mute and sanguinary mood: of beings undergoing a harmony of ultimate demand and supply.

Nothing is strange here. It is an ordinary town. A common pulse. A deep mineral resource. A consummation of the obvious.

A way of life.

the blue rental

LINGUISTIC

DUPLEX

/on the abduction and murder of Polly Klaas, October 1993/

du plex   Latin   double
"A house divided into two living units"

lingua   Latin   language, tongue
"The science of language; the study of the
nature and structure of human speech"

double tongue
                    / double talk
tongue double
                    / shadow speech
                    Speech shadow
                    stand-in
            doppelganger words

"the stunned headlong certainty that precedes
talking in tongues...."
                    Thomas Pynchon VINELAND

CALCIUM
        a silvery metallic element that occurs in bone, shells,

limestone and gypsum, and forms compounds used to
make plaster, quicklime, cement, and metallurgic
and electronic materials.
atomic number   20
atomic weight   40.08
symbol   Ca

L   calx   lime, limestone   Gk   khalix   pebble

RADIO

the use of electromagnetic waves in the approximate
frequency range from 10 kilocycles/second to 300,000
megacycles/second to transmit or receive electric
signals without wires connecting the points of
transmission and reception
communication of audible signals, such as music,
encoded in electromagnetic waves so transmitted and
received
transmission of programs for the public by this means;
radio broadcast
the equipment used for transmitting or receiving
radio signals
adj   of or sent by radio   of or using oscillations
of radio frequency
verb   to transmit a message to, or communicate
with, by radio

short for RADIOTELEGRAPHY

Latin   radix   root
Latin   radius   spoke of a wheel, ray

TONGUE

"....the arrangement of Cro-Magnon man's oral and
nasal cavities, his longer pharynx – the section of
throat just above the vocal cords – and the
flexibility of his tongue enabled him to shape and
project sounds over a much wider range, and much
more rapidly, than early humans could.
His superior vocalizing powers were gained at one
big expense, however: modern man is the only creature
who can choke to death on food caught in his wind-
pipe, because his longer pharynx must do double duty
as the route to his alimentary canal."
                    CRO-MAGNON MAN, Tom Prideaux Books
                    The Emergence of Man. Time-Life
                    NYC 1973 Time Inc.

the blue rental

1. her flowers

the sounds pass thru our walls big chambers of the heart
we live in bodies as we live in rooms with numbers the street
names of each face in bathroom mirrors and the radio does not
stop at her wall but permutes my membrane sound is more like
blood than anything it pulses in and out of shapes red splash
of music in the street spilled news from a distant hemorrhage
pain crushed cicadas silence
midnight
rubbing legs thighs together are the walls permeable
growing,ruptured petals of, the children explode and blossom
stain of all hearts

her mother came from she came from i came from
earth flesh time

the walls are thin to hear everything. kids scream beyond 3 of
them jump on beds laugh friends 4 more happy sound to be grateful
for the radio is electric nervous thread   transgenetic history
stitches her space singing TexMex into my space in single body of
musical air country disco rock mariachi rodeo guitar needles of
dust beer all the machines are drunk outside cruise transam in the
small sleep street echotunnel of cottonwood and shadow thick adobe
walls Mexican weekend the boombox occasionally glides by it is not
poetry but all surrounding time space this is our flesh (Aztec
Mayan Irish German)tangled roots,spliced all erupting   here
record of flesh mother 3 kids her mother in the other house side
heavy sucked by gravity back to earth recovering breast cancer
surgery chemo keeps the children while her daughter goes to class
nursing credential broken down brown car install beeping siren
when ex-boyfriend ex-husband ex-everything attempts to break inside
the night to sleep weep do some creepy thing between 2 a.m. and
dawn   over and over
the siren goes off alone,in the night malfunctions it is lonely

her kids are fine,sweet 5,6 11 she has a daughter on the edge
of exploding   petals
i had,have a daughter, daughters i was,she was we were once all
ways   those flowers

long ago, the stories go the mother air the song of water walls of
inner dark,cool   the bread was made, the walls of hearts the
children jumped up and down,played   happy sound
long ago, we hear on the radio

that is from time: genetic codes come from: dial,static,song   the
meteor crash Yucatan dinosaur   leaves of sacred books burn flesh
piles up in histories   as bodies
abducted from one dream   dumped in another generations low
rent 8 plastic body bags aluminum beercans in the yard
otherwise exhausted of grass the exhusbands junked Mercury the
exboyfriends threats of serious trouble
they come about 3 a.m. after the bars close drunken baskets of
laundromat shirts pants socks underwear hang in stupors along the
clothesline pinned like no woman ever hung out to dry you know
it is an act of revenge in the morning the ex-mans laundry
like one hundred crows overhung on the sour lines
and they hang there for a week and the exboyfriend cocaine
pissed comes by and rehangs them in strange and sinister ways
e.g. pinning 4 shirts together in one place, while pants are
split with one broken, kicked-out   frayed leg
dangling now in the dust   three weeks of this
and banging on walls shouts screams   rocks and full beercans
thrown at the house predawn phonecalls red swirling splash of
rotating copcar waking the interior walls like nightmare thrown
blood heart attack of the street
and sometime between midnite and dawn he is on the roof stumbling
and stomping drunk and coke high all over the victorian shingles
and this is a language
this is the way they talk

poetry of the exploding   body

rages lusts terrors revenges semiotic idiotics wired psychotics
barrio   ghetto far hotel suburb quiet neighborhood night
radio men

our children (3) jump and scream to the same machine
the heart is wired to receive   everything

and to live here under the same roof is they say a woman in the

world of everywhere is bleeding   i live, i lived i will live
poverty of flesh unites us   the radio,sound rips interior walls
open   we tape, patch glue sew stitch get thru another the
wound opens again   like clockwork, of the heart ticking

bombs explode, Ireland Mexico gaslines,cities airplanes   messages
on the radio, not here   only scattered gunfire of laughter
driving by drunk, post-midnite
or a bullet thru the heart, which was an accident
the kids tell of it next day, click blam spray red flowers
at school

the child is crying why why is the sound of a little girl
blubbering whimpering worse
                                            leaking thru the walls
like a curse of blood the implicit meaning inside some
wallpaper mold blood ink writing time large yellowbrown
stains insects wings thus reading books open
to some discourse
                                    intercourse beer parties firecrackers
night exploding all such red flowers

on the other side i sit inside cool a cool highceilinged spacious
dark room filled with boxes of my books,life and the radio on
timespace acoustic sandwich between them i am the one in the middle
who makes noise here tatatat a typewriter shoved against their flesh
wall driveby random bullets tatatat a joyride it was an accident
keeps the baby from sleep in the afternoon she is not a baby but
5 years old but she screams tantrums gets revenge (for what?)

(my daughter screamed,writhed from allergies do they scream after
breakfast cereals red food dye caramel color lollipops the one who
was hurt tho didn't scream. one wonders why she didn't scream. we
need to tell them: there is a right to do so)

in the heart of 3 pm street of radio cruise saturdays planet of somewhere
dry times i wish i could type silent as a fly specks the wall with
black indelible feet this attitude appropriate but it is a typewriter
older than all of us Remie Scout original thinker solid crisp as the

poet who sent it to me from his deceased fathers memory
"from the same company that makes the rifles!"
he said.
ratatatat a dream-by shouting

and here it comes crackling thru the fine night insect scratching
inside the walls tonight radio television news 1000 miles away? the
blood begins to leak from the stained paper of the walls which do
not stop the flow of sound pulse information weeping agony inside
this big chambered heart of our hearing.night

Petaluma   you know the flowers of the mother who is everywhere
so torn and weeping

BOOMBOX: somebodys machine heart

some big machine heart slides slowly down the street of silence
sweat cicadas transam yearning

murdering. of flowers

we are all tuned to it,cannot escape
(deaf, you hear it pounding inside a skull, hemorrhage as seed
rattles,scratches in a box of night vibrations travel along the nerves
who bloom,who sing
the pain in everyone

the heart is dialed to receive her. everything. cannot escape

Polly and 2 friends were playing PERFECT MATCH when Davis appeared
in her room with a knife.
"where are your valuables" he asked
she was the valuable. she showed him her piggy bank with $20
girl-earned dollars

EVIL IS A TRANCE in which he took her from her life with knives
into the darkness drove her telling if they screamed hed kill
them all.
she was alive he said when police stopped him hidden,nearby in the
bushes Davis says he was "mystified she didnt scream"

the blue rental

(the one who screams on the other side i think of birds in some
jungle some existences are violent like red shrieks of birds flying
upward into green lucid consciousness
but purple,the blood of brutal. mutation of the young)

was she bound and gagged? not bound not gagged? no yes no cant
remember so deranged drugged swollen into monster god cant remember
why she didnt logically scream
out of such terror
(we scream logically upward,birds in flight)

woman in the audience: was she strangled or was she stabbed
her father does not listen to the radio no tv news since She is dead,
is all he can say. a sweatshirt with blood on it found whose?
strangled stabbed beaten surely this is America we have a choice

we are mystified the police were mystified listening to the wrong
radio frequency of life/death do not hear the allpoints
bulletin SCREAMING TO ALL POINTS OF THE EARTH

he was mystified we are mystified the parole board let him out
on Parole   PAROLE is WORD on his word on the word on words of
over and over let him out 8 years into a 16 year sentence for
doing the same thing MYSTIFIED over and over and over
this is his Word

EVIL is a trance   all the psychokillers are among us loose
running in and out of our minds our eyes bleeding from our genital
mouths we open our mouths to scream BUT WE ARE MYSTIFIED WE
MAKE NO SOUND we open our children as wallets to give our flowers
of cherished wealth to robbers we offer our children as
propitiation on the cold autopsy laps of the gods

the young girls Kate and Gillian see him clearly describe him
uncannily the police drawing is frightening in its closeness
to his eyes the police pick him up drunk driving a month later
and do not see it

WE ARE MYSTIFIED THEY DO NOT SEE IT THEY DO NOT SCREAM
the woman calls the police a trespasser on her land she hears
she sees she noticed something strange she finds 2 months later

bloody sweatshirt on her land her INSTINCT was clear was so
close to his crime WE ARE MYSTIFIED WE SEE WE HEAR WE
    SMELL SOME BLOOD
OF ATROCITY but we do not scream

on Parole   Parole is word on his word on the word on words of
experts of GOD he is captured and released and captured and released
and he feels "a warm glow" a "release" of tension
over and over and over

so he wonders why she didnt scream TAKE THE LAW INTO HER OWN HANDS
at knife point hed taken her from her life telling her and 2 friends
that if they screamed hed kill her mother and her little sister
sleeping in the next room
THAT IF THEY SCREAMED hed kill them all

and this is his power his power was in the Good Behavior of young girls

NOT TO SCREAM she took in silence his evil thus to spare preserve
flowering   these others

(his rage,behind walls swollen purple existential tongue, strangled
impotence inside some skull,wall squirming mind of a psycho killer
always laying back in his prison cell
passive empty masturbatory
with good behavior
        is that no matter what he does,she is alive remains living
true beauty innocent brave even in horrid death his infliction
does not deform her it is his face only,always his foetid stink
breathing of himself behind this wall he rots exiled from,denied
(her flowers)

and he is closed up behind a strong wall with all the institutions
of men judge police lawyer parole dictionary god
professionals who Profess words who speak PAROLE the oath of words
to uphold the rule of
to uphold his dick while he does it again and over and again
mystified
she does not scream

why young girls? experts media ask experts answer BECAUSE IT IS
SO EASY   so easy bend down rip up handfuls of flowers from such an

the blue rental

earth designated   as YOURS

by god the experts the experts claim to know what is Good Behavior

he smirks   200 pounds   he is among prisoners cops lawyers judges
parole boards psychosocial workers   a big man

2. calcium

the radio speaks   machines in one room suffering is another   a
thought may scream blood burst wall,pipes root   solitude of all throats
they are not heard   no one sits with open mouth gagged teeth gone
choked by staring at life   screams   the machinery tells us   is
not heard

he is   among (Time)   a Big Man

prison) brain of toilets,stench overspill   forced anus
torture cells is his home
                              shit is of the air of his mind he breathes
(flowering)all life as dirtied .political
dynamics of male fear they cannot deal with terror of, each
other this realization of *terra* terror testosterone fathers to sons
priests to boys punk factories armies gangs to the alone   what
they do,each other   over and over   closed
up skull,fist groin institutions of groins make BigMen make the
otherWOMAN fuck each other 200 million sperm make A WOMAN
bleed humiliation he feels a GLOW and
RELEASE this PRISON(lived in a trailer 3rd child of 5 unwanted abused
by father left alone
home of pain(locked,mind)
                              he is valuable there
wallet,semen   testimony muscle hung dick swollen steroids alcohol
dope gods men big,mean as gods with urge INFLICT)Men MAKE a
WOMAN   push in,his fear   open her eyes
the victim chosen,weaker given them by(God,men,law reason,custom
as offerings little fingers   scratch   the hideous itch   that
Terror fill up the eyes of earth
TO MAKE A WOMAN   she wants it

prison(is numbered,scum EMPTY
alone)they feed him videos of infant sex sodomy on boys pale girls
just as they flower first months of menstrual blood and are
acutely sensitive then to their bodies the
intrusions of alien males and thus   (as a child hurt so naked by
shame)he lays back on his bunk fantasizing sour yellow fingers
insert into innocence   absence,evil,pain it is the
perfect time
maximization of fear in their eyes   to become
female   be Punished for it
                              (the god of Justice swells   glows
by thick finger rancid penile projection of a smile,disease
selfdisgust BigSickMan fear which can be exorcised   into eyes of
flowers
firstblood   others
then he is value   in prison(avenged) onPain
if he could do it with a dirty knifeblade his sour razor a
beer bottle a rifle his soldiers bayonet his fathers belt buckle
raise welts on her petal flesh if he could do it with the
vomiting tip of nose nosebleed childhood nosebrain stem of a
species which alone lusts to mutilate its young not
food not reproduce another
not reproduce another in her place (he wore a condom)but THE
PUNISHMENT OF FLESH ON FLESH FOR BEING
                  (alive,beyond wall this hard brain who is living
i will make Terror fill up Her Eyes
rip
unimprisoned life   ,make a *woman*

"are we god?"
ask the judges   who release him

experts,who make money in america   lawyers judges   experts
of man locked up in prison of men   big business all down the
line $25,000 one male one small cell release him(Parole)$500,000
watch him if he keeps his Word   maltliquor speed nicotine pornflick
coke cruise unemployed cars upon the sullen streets   stalk,surveille
hang out hangout his dick on corners,frontseats expose solicit
                  the offering of flesh by god to fix this,hungering
small lost handfuls of children or blood of animals which
pay which will pay for prison   mind,of men

the blue rental

over and over

he is mystified   "glow" "release"
he told them   he announces to Parole Boards over and over
"considered to be considerably dangerous to others,especially women
. . .if released,he is certain to resume his pattern of behavior"
mystified they know what he is YOU KNOW WHAT I AM I DO I
        GAVE MY
WORD 8 years imprisoned lifetimes Tensionsquirming building to
do it and they open the doors
and they open the doors RELEASE him   glowing
spurt of luminous sperm

he says they want it
vicarious Glow and RELEASE   .the experts
voices tell him. strangle hurt   because they want him to
do it Women ask for it   unspoken female words,of
luminous singing
are we god?
ask judges   "there was no reason to keep him"

ARE WE GOD asks the weenie judge who is paid as a god with
godlike powers over us the blows of BigMen kicks bruises cuts rapes
strangulations knifethrusts Vengeance of BigMen,little men
who give the Word
voices tell him   all vicarious men systems of cons judges hard balls
gods paid by Your Dollar tax VA SSI corrections budget payroll
rehab make such men release them upon all the soft neighborhoods
penal pensions emptiness nothing to do but
the virginal thighs of neighborhoods   where women,pale
whores girls wait waiting wanting criminal
violation
it is not violation they want it
he does not Violate His PAROLE because he already told them:
Voices ,in explosions of Worlds,8 years   dreams of putrid cells,a
life dead fantasies of nasty things you watch you want but
cannot i exist ,
EXPLODE then as a god   ,released   incandescent sperm
flood eyes,mouth vaginas of them   i Glow(fluorescent tubes,steel
stink of fear bodies of boys   forced,shove in
all the institutions   of pain my swollen MEMBER clubs and Expertise
of punishment

they wait   frontporches office doorways bedrooms bathtubs school
swing cradle gardens   are silent   i hear them   tell me
do things to them   GIVE MY WORD the voices sing

/LINGUISTIC GLOSS,or the Shining Tongue of Madness/

now we fly thru a wall,limestone text once colors of animals blue
ochre coal shapes of radio time now stain spread as bruises hemorrhage
of mind,blood is flying
it was once a cave of echoes and the skull,of luminous pictures
he couldve been i hear them
HE DOES NOT REMEMBER DOING IT HE DID NOT KNOW HER NAME

it is not of words it is in syntax,the bone
it was a skull of intention, reverence of animals
the head bangs walls sentences of simple blood all secondthoughts are
gone until flying thru deep,moist textures now bright red pages
dripping HE DOES NOT EVEN REMEMBER HE WAS NOT EVEN THERE

make men sick with gods,imprisoned drug them to survive it give them
women animals children to explode in Human Civilization

he could be
he couldve been
once as a hunter,artist spits luminous things on walls(flickering
light,the blue horse ,bison stunned wizard her awesome cunt
in walls,my skull i hear them   limbs hearts dreams connections   the
radio is screaming she is crazy brain wires leak,all the broken
things are dangling

lawyers judges physicians dentists electrical engineers airline pilots
are professions wellpaid in america the Experts who are of our
thought body smiles,good digestion   LIGHT   who climb excitable air
to make a civilization of us
                    they spit luminous things on walls   flickering
music blue horses, torsion   necklace of teeth bird wizard her
womb of all forms
                    (caves,echoesHistory we
hear   another room,beyond Time as rental bone
CroMagnon luminous spewer of beasts on walls,becoming mans cathedrals

the blue rental

the perfect Chinese horse Lascaux the gods now are flying
his arms covered with tattoos,blue hallucinating flesh
he couldve been something something

speed sex psychochemistry psychometrics dirty gas can of brainstemspasm
BOOM BOX compulsions
he couldve been
he couldve been   a contender   yah yah yah
but HE WAS NOT THERE he is not
she is not
someone
goes by,rips out the heart,cut   bleeding   cannot escape
the last thing she saw of earth was his face   eyes bulged,the BigMans
purple tongue
                (her scream,inside   all skulls knowledge,words
those paid for Justice are not screaming   )catacombs of lost in dark,
fear pain   health law light,good ambition
make men crazy with sick religion drug them to get thru it give
them women little girls to explode in WESTERN CIVILIZATION
a World soars in murals of air
i am a crazy old woman

women who nurse children
loony,old   not experts in anything
locked by walls also,bad nutrition teeth gone poetry,locked up in
rental rooms,houses we scream at(wallpaper,dead people,institutions of
dull cabbage)kids laundry radios nothing at all no experts
to be rich in america   expert in law health teeth sheer electric
flight
and nowhere are so useless here the women unauthorized to speak
schools libraries spines (the public mind) chronic malnutrition   nurse
3 children 9 years welfare calcium lost to poetry
do not consider vocations of women(who reproduce: time space
engineers doctors lawyers and teeth)
poor women reproduce. crime and prison
(this is linoleum buildup they sd this is thinking too hard   over
and over   to no end)
PRISONERS   lawyers judges parole officers are gods,poets
gnaw on rocks "poor dental hygiene" all the duplex floors,kitchen
bathroom bedrooms stained linoleum (how to get dentures among the

poor, commit crime go to prison
poor men have more teeth,more crime than poor women
are we gods

)we watch on tv,in state prison they throw their plates on the floor
roastbeef mashed potatoes peas the hugemuscled men throw it
on the floor,not enough protein for them $18 per prisoner per day for
criminal protein 50 cents per meal per person AFDC women and children
walls are cement,lies accretions of Time its rotting grin,decay
of speech erosion lexicon, the walls are smug expertise,inertia
flushed excreta of wellpaid bone
$25,000 year per prisoner in a small double cell
$60-100 per day per inmate local jail

in Pelican Bay maximum security prison men claim they are
unnaturally punished isolated in cells cold and terrible as the grave
say they are inhumanly confined there WE ARE THE VICTIMS
forced,anal   VICTIM SHIT   locked
inside, cruel caves of,systems of Mind   (CRIMEN: the word for
crime,verdict judgment is the same CRIMEN,his Cry of Pain)
experts the experts
know what is the grave   cold final brutal   how to get around it
(Richard Allen Davis complained   his nightly sleep was interrupted by
screams,howls of fellow prisoners,then he howled with toothache
and got a root canal,very expensive   and his public defense
lawyer required complete dental work,top and bottom, before he
could begin to speak   the Words of a trial)
welltrained in PeckingOrder   guns mace naked ass SM control
steel lockup pod limbic systems swollen bureaucrazies boiled death as a
punks broth,beaten selfpity excremental video psychoProd   forced
anal punisher PUNISH HER (revenge: earth left him alone   small
lost afraid   at the mercy of men)
and another says   VICTIM SHIT what is all this VICTIM SHIT i am
a good guy   if he does not overly rape or kill
other men in prison   or the judge,or
the experts   this is good behavior   locked up forever,with
grown men   he is safe
Experts   wellpaid,wives children mortgages   secure on the other side
shuffling,paper stale thought dull words jargon of expertise
"Positive Psychiatric Report" "Model Prisoner" "Parole Release"
words sentences paragraphs monographs whitenoise SHITNOSE

the blue rental

timeserving of the gods
they dont see him coming
                              (experts,dont see him coming
blood all over the naked child

captured on Coyote Reservation, Davis   in a house,living
room maybe a linoleum floor   with shagrug or striped blanket a
coffeetable with a human skull on it   like an ashtray   he smirked and
laughed giving impression he   worked for Death
take law into our own hands,SCREAM   if not they must want it
this way

Ellie Nesler shoots her childs molester (convicted once,released)
in the courthouse brain Judge Polley makes Law and Order
decision SENTENCES her to 10 years prison diagnosed TerminalBreast
Cancer she has 5 years to live that means with Good Behavior she
could get out in 5 years
Death will Parole her

Death keeps its Word

Expert to the bone,Spinal determinant ,appears to us to insist without
you cant stand up   (they appear to but sit,process compute count our
rotting bone   flying flying thru time taste the, putrid discourse   )
altho this would appear true on "material" plane it posits a (perhaps?)
problematic hierarchy of bones which some deconstruct of Academic
feminisms would seek to dissolve,extract dematerialize ESSENCE as if
one is not (thinking,feeling geologic)mother authorized to have opinions
of blood
DETERMINISM of "reality" poses the dilemma we must accept itsPrefab
definitions or redefine them,extantSelves suggest some dualistic
either/or choice of multioptional universe in theoretical opportunities
rare discourse of course which does pay rent for its practitioners.but we
have left the field of potential,as collapsing bones:we have left the
room where stench of actual perpetration chokes and gags us:do we
are we have we not argue from strange existence being alive viz that
if spines collapse in MEANING the inferential crux of context is one
cant stand up (talk,back,fight,shake nerves knots of fist explosion
thru the World as blood flew)or in the property of trees gagged with

her own red tights and flying,flying red bird wings up   and
away such Expert Design,events   and ergo some Determinism
(terminUS)seems appears subtextual subposited even tho we rush
with enormous linguistic erasures to subvert   (the flow upwards of
vast departures the floorboards of this department   )where Experts
slaver,drool on their knees like naked dogs
(i scrub i scrub i scour i cannot clean the floors,walls ears of this
apartment the radio with one long stationary,expanding cry
ratatatat ratatatat ratatatatat ratatatatatatat ratatthedoor
the howl of men as Dogs sniffing rectums of their own Law   ,Experts
if admit then practice of spinalDeterentermination does said praxis
say it lead us into what enormous construal as BIOLOGIC ONTOLOGY
which stigmaticText,critique suggests meets its reversal (variable?)in
experiential equivalent oppositional appearance of wholly inert,
determining something   something
are we gods?

abstract ,impassive ,impotent   ,laid back STARE AT THE WALL
viz,i.e., *praxis of paralysis* mans law emerges caves to retrieve the
unopposed terms of discourse with their discredited matrix bringing us
back,where we are   stained,foul mattress the stench of
his cell   to move or to be unable to move or to be unable to rise from
the floor seems to posit some DETER/Termination of an END of a
prior intent or dream of NATURE
EXPLOSIONS OF STARS BODIES OF STARS   INTO OUR
FORMS   THOUGHT   CAVES   AND SHAPES OF CALCIUM
                    (the echoes of such event)

release RELEASE him over and over to GLOW in the shining bloodstream
of   all   night
do they not Want This, EVERYONE? forever? forever?

consider the massive headtrips sustainable by an economy of abundance
grotesquely imbalanced in the direction of funded abstractions and their
subtextualized careers in referential delineation from the great exterior
masses of apparent "material" or "real" situations such as living bodies
germ veins garbage cars investment brokerage pipe corrosions(*want
this*, EVERYONE WANTS THIS wait for vicarious release this Evil
tension)   influxions of indifferent definitions of sewage and related
contaminations into the specifiably "cleansed" or unsubliminal random
debouche of professionals would seem to suggest whatever possible
on paper in mind IS doable,eatable regardless withholding the referent

nonconsiderial world or responding agonies or,i.e.   *dream on thy sheer
linguistic lingerie tongue exercise* to DREAM is not possible,alive

but twists itself elsewhere that is the bones of actual screams and
utter hallucinated flux of blood discourse poetry clots choke and thick
phlegm serum of a vision from mouths nostrils anuses of those unable
refusing to vomit huge complexes,oceans into coke bottles or other
(similar or oppositional)units of oral retension,reductive dimension
(books) MLA Journals Feminist Studies bloody periodicals (critiques
due mal tete feminine du bouche bourgeois   )
(because we are so TrulyFine above it all NOT ANIMALS repeat we are
not "beasts" BiologicDeterminism do not apply we are Abstract beyond
the neck,our careers are such crimes are senseless "monstrous" *de trop*
nor are we gods?)

subterefuge,of SYNTAX are so many hiding underground   caverns
of the hunted Quasimodo   (ars longa vita brevis:so long,suckers   )
subterranean rivers of resultant hells are powerful ARE flowing and
question whether attack on "sin" is even relevant to the field of
tortured visions *in situo* now a plaza of burning flesh seems almost
materially pertinent but somehow abysmally overdone in "fact"

what are the lucrative industries of pain,in america   CRIME DISEASE
TOOTHLESS RAGE EXPLODING NERVES LOCKED UP IN WALLS
MADNESS   (there are wings of terrific metals,to fly away
excluding those who play games with balls cunts,titties   giant
$port$ figures   lest we be left sick toothless without entertainment
lawless cold hungry without voice   alone   deaf in the dark
unable to fly
yr Taxes pay for EVERYTHING
he doesnt even remember being

we can go on like this forever do you want to stop?
"want" "stop" "forever" "you" "i" "go" "we" can like this go on to
there is a tax on sin.   it is called Time. and SIN is WITHOUT,meaning
forever.
the child is dead

and those who make academic living selfresearchingly breaking down
one universe,world of DISCOURSE into others must bleed well have a
genius,POETRY to replace it with time more Real or if not if they
cannot (expertise:paralysis) shut up shut up shut up leave move our

barbara mor

bloody screaming thru walls permeate solid flesh compartments(cells of
terrible rooms)where my heart is screaming

thus conclusions become titles demonstrate models   circle of
deadeye dogs in cosmos of tailinterrogating "closure" which is not
closed,closes nothing but a more problemautomatic theoremetic
palpable grim intermuttent pain in the ass (of dogs,scAvengers of the
rubble that is left, that is, but also the mind OPEN ALL NIGHT 24
HOURS ,who speaks of, unauthorized weariness).
                    linoleum buildup,bAnal employment of
statistical mediocrities as institutes of compulsion who is punked who
punks who gets it in the assTO MAKE OF THE UNIVERSE A
SHITHOLE Big Man
say it. the more Latinate the more Lies

:toward a Paradigm (phoneme? chakra? mode of discourse? 20 cents?)
those who speak correctly who are authorized to speak,they are the
ones with Teeth (degrees of,credit cards careers ,medical
and dental coverage)
i have none
she is crazy

so she goes to get medical/dental care (spine nodes skin skull teeth)
and there is none she is told woman old poor writes books no coverage
has been homeless, she is crazy "we have reason to think you suffer from
mental/emotional disturbance" and when she says no they send PhD of
psychology to her door to test her mind
refuses screams on payphone returns forms go to hell disappears at
appointed time they break into suspects house to investigate living
arrangements find on bathroom mirror and adjoining wall yellow stickon
paper squares with handscrawled messages saying FEED CHINA, this
constitutes evidence she is crazy they obtain bench warrant to seize
her person remove her to the local psychiatric detention center where
upon her delusionally outraged protest she is injected with sufficient
grains of sand of thorazine to shut her up
that the duplex neighbor ex-man besieged cancer mother 3 children
had recently obtained a 2 year old female partChow dog named "China"
who chained outside in position to defend the property from intruders
drunk cokehead excon boyfriends crazy exhusband all their driveby

84

relatives randomly spewing beercans bullets revenge rocks thru 2 a.m.
car windows at yr sleeping eyes was earlier that day upon leaving for
3 day visit to Arizona sister said neighbor requests subject to "feed
the dog" upon which agreed and left a key to obtain bag dogfood on
jumbled backporch behind screendoor,thus notes left by subject to
remind self subject to do task which eventuated in her removal from her
life and "literary work" and relocate in permanent drugged brain state
of mental asylum for the humanly delusional   (i.e. one deranged
enough to leave herself notes reminding self to provide nourishment
for an Asian nation of some 3 billion souls when the woman obviously
and verifiably did not have wherewithal essentially to feed herself)
n.b.: did subject not apply (unsuccessfully) for public assistance?

she is not a billion years old she is notRoot&flower ofHistory is not
the skull inside wall some woman sings crazy "CRAZY" on radio of her
destiny as plane(small,private) goes down in swift flames
and now she screams at her kids SHUT UP I CANT SLEEP I CANT THINK she
cant study i am typing ratatat they yell,shriek jump up and down I WILL
BEAT THE SHIT OUT OF YOU DAMNIT I MEAN IT

scream i scream we are screaming the radio squeezes   boombox
machine heart   a terrible noise   we cant breathe
we are the ones with meaning   who mean it it is not blood,crazy women
pleasure "jouissance" equal privilege perfume ad satisfy one wants the
mass commercial TrueRomance(only a 6pack drunk to numb the
sufficient pain) one wants SOLELY space time a partial modem of
intelligent, space,time quiet LUMINOUS which inour Expert Discourse of
need is "problematic"
duplex singlemother three kids (5 6 11) with a typewriter battering
uptight next to the paper thin bedroom wall the cheapest one can get and
still no one can afford it   and thus the subject exteriorizes into
malignant typocentric neighborhoods of anecdotal noise and
migraine interrogation wonder resultant appropriation futures this waxy
buildup (we go on like this forever do you want to stop

and now the mother is dying postsurgery pain chest hips they
told her FAT lose weight feel better about yourself surgical
oncologist expert she speaks no english speaks nothing but
stolid endurance poverty mother of much flesh not enough the
doctor wanted $1000 more not covered by coverage of plans of
world of the night the coverage of night is very deep and quiet
here she is dying now tumor into chest bones and hips and the

barbara mor

daughter drops out of nursing school to care for and who will
sit 3 children while she studies or works the only place that
can afford the Baptist Bible Camp School bus takes them
off to play and make known to them GodsWill the mother riddled
now bullets of cancer rapidly spread the driveby shooting of
experts of the experts
death

a phone rings on the other side that is the Universe,says STOP
message message heard received message flying thru the wall as its
exploding particles
(or: is the universe linguistic? holographique? Rubiks Cube of endless
true infinite expanding despite not being able to afford the rent
duplex a p a r t m e n t s...?   deepart   meants mentis
the typography of department is (re: art meant) on the shadow side of
stars
the origin of our universe is on the darkside of our stars

3. shelter

on the west coast Ireland   before radio before tv one could
stand there clear daylight once every 7 years see luminous picture
around globe over atlantic a woman hanging white laundry in
an alley in Brazil
and hear an incredible singing
mayan faces african drums washed up on the soft beach huge
messages
air so clear you could hear,see   voyage of a world
around itself   a biologic singing,clairvoyant   atmosphere of
   all story

these were the happy isles, Hy Brasil (america) transmit on
waves of the deep sea television our eyes immigrant radio distances
ratatatat of random typewriters
always legends,news reports of the clean land beyond

i was born in a duplex conceived my first years a duplex on
the pacific ocean my father selfemployed radio repair 1936

the blue rental

with small converted garage shop on one side,and nextdoor
the other living unit was a medium the gypsy they said she
conducted seances in the dark rooms next to my conception
and sleep and infant dream as i grew into this telepathic
wiring   hearing seeing
what happens in the dark

what speaks the dark

             red tights, girls
             knotted,a gag   mans bloody sweatshirt
             tape   a condom
             he used a condom
             she was alive then,he said   among
             good earth, and trees
             she did not scream

the ritual of lost men discover america men with nothing to do
but move around lost they want to eat   lust   swell the
flesh they have betrayed once given them they now believe as the
punishment we deserve they are not of a Devil they are of
Themselves,lost   sick masturbatory crazed they penis they
punish the female perhaps because she gives them birth

drops them into water,dirt soiled cloth howling   animals

are we gods?

invention of cars men cruising deep pornographies of oil
insomnias the eyes of dead fish
cruising by young girls laughing on bicycles show them yr
sour unzipped lap sick hands masturbating tumescence of losers
fish eyes dead eyes 200 million sperm per come oozes to the rotten
bottom end of the world the sea receives foam waste residue release
of Time
into all eyes

he used a condom
closed up inside foul car exoskeletal cruising insect of squirming
Xs X-rate techno images dials of videos the glass of his eyes

we see so closely into thru we cruise the mutilated girls
of landscape
whoever stood up from worms to be human now lie down again to sleep
nothing to do but stalk the fresh dreams of neighborhoods that they
are innocent unarmed civilian flesh of living that anything
could be clean alive outside dark windows of empty eyes
beyond him his fingers have not squeezed with sperm anything beyond
untouched undirtied violated by masturbations of his
dreams

hear the distant transmissions of dreams

                              waste of young girls bright minds victory
                              of sperm explosions testicle revenge
                              the sour masturbations of killers over us
                              useless men
the one who screams on the other side i think of birds in jungle
flight some existences are ludic,consciousness   a violent red
shriek of one bird flying inside a skull,wall

he used a condom
what in gods name for
not to reproduce himself on the other side of Death

        only in prison,is shelter from evil
        behind some wall,closed up utterly alone
        or,where he is among men   so evil as he
        or men who are not innocent, but love the desperation of
        exploding flowers

        no child no woman beyond his solitude   selfdisgust becomes revenge
        only with opening of flowers,spring him
        release him let him out to do it again
        revenge of man of flesh for the Eve of being,flesh
        which he has made of it   (us,this)
        only in prison,is shelter
        closed up inside his terrible wall,alone teeth forehead
        against
        my skull

the blue rental

A BULLET THRU THE BRAIN   WHAT YOU GIVE TO ANY SICK
ANIMAL EVEN THE FAMILY DOG IF IT BECOMES RABID   NOT
LET OUT ON THE HUMAN STREETS TO BITE AGAIN

they seem to be having trouble enacting justice
give him to me give him to crazy old women the witches of
justice i will spread his legs arms stake him naked
to the public earth   upon her last place
i will with my poetry hand cut off his dick
scrotum shave him menstrual bloody pubic hair render him
bare and raw as a little girl spreadeagled shove
his genitals in his mouth
so he does not scream
then standing back i invite the community of men
to do him   all they dream of scheme is dick in a hole dick in a
hole dick in a hole let every man come forward one
by one shove sticks rods bayonets police batons broken
bottles ram his asshole jam the naked blood hole i
have made into him (hell) until they have had their fill
killer dick shove in a bloody hole
once and for all

until they weary,sick of selves
what they do what they have done
what he does for all of them   vicarious revenge
                              systems of rapers
                          expertise of ravaged flowers
for they know not what they do is a lie all living things
know what we do
                (tell me of yr sad life,i listen)
and then i stand with a bloody knife hand
raised up,dripping   i say *next*?

the shelter in Tucson many homeless women their children my first
night i remember the young girl 10, 11 so eager polite pressed close
to me on couch a FAMILY CIRCLE open to an article on cutting paper
flowers, i told her of the fiesta of many nations i'd seen with
my daughter who was her age, the Polish exhibit a woman scissoring

incredible cathedral windows,fireworks of flowers,birds at the
courthouse plaza outside, given to the children
her name was Sherlyn Karen Shondra i cant remember Cathleen Sara
Polly   it was Sheila
so eager polite i knew she was frightened, her mother homeless
nicotine thin frayedged at the mercy of streets habitual men
they were on their way to Phoenix she said they were going to have
an apartment a place to live she'd go to school
she was so glad to sit with me, stay, pressed against my body the
glossy magazine spread open on her lap and mine,questions questions
keeping me there discussing Flower Cutting Paper Flowers a
Polish Folk Art did you see this how do they do this and this she
trembled with an eagerness,shining with what i learned to know
was Terror
in the news report the mothers exboyfriend just went up the stairs
of the new apartment they were moving into opened fire as they say
a gun(opening of red flowers) wounded the mother,killed the
girl a sudden red bloom appeared in her chest her eyes wide
i knew she was afraid we were all afraid i could do nothing her
mother came into the room appeared from shadows pulled her away a
deranged look at me suspicious HOMELESS WITH A HOPELESS
WEAK POOR MOTHER THE THINGS SHE'D ALREADY HAD
DONE TO HER THE THINGS SHE FEARED WOULD HAPPEN
i could do nothing
but feel her glistening eagerness to know EVERYTHING about
cut paper flowers before she was dragged off to the dark

no Shondra was the one i last saw sitting on a toilet the open door,

she was young half indian from the northwest glistening pretty
but a scar diagonal across her face from cheekbone to jaw because
drugs alcohol because they took away her children she abandoned

her boyfriend took her down to the dry river bank camps where she
was gangbanged by all the homeless men there *fucked in the ass*
i heard them joke of it later with her boyfriend, she wasnt around

the last time i saw her hunched on a toilet legs sprawled open
flushed with lightbulb the fenced junkyard after midnite the needle in
her arm she was nodding the line of men,5-7 of them slouched away
from this little shrine into the darkness, waiting

the blue rental

* * * * * * * * * *

Quotes from 1978 Psychiatric Report on Richard Allen Davis, a sealed
    document ordered unsealed after Jan 27, 1994 ABC PRIMETIME
    covered the Polly Klaas kidnapping and murder.

A US NEWS & WORLD REPORT essay by John Leo, "Dealing with
    Career Predators" (April 11, 1994) quoted a criminologist's
    description of R. A. Davis as "a monstrous personality."

When asked why R. A. Davis was released after serving only 8 years of
    a 16 year sentence for violet abduction & sexual assault, with a
    psychiatric assessment record of being "considerably dangerous to
    others, especially women" along with a warning that "if released,
    he is certain to resume his pattern of behavior," the release judges
    responded "there was no reason to keep him" & "are we god?"

"What is all this VICTIM SHIT....I'm a good guy" quote from a CBS
    48 Hours report (March 9, 1994) on parolee Russell Obremski.
    Obremski raped and murdered an 8-month pregnant woman; in
    flight, he kidnapped, raped and murdered another mother of 2.
    Given "Two Life Sentences" he was released in November 1993
    after serving 24 years in prison. A few months later, Obremski
    was arrested & indicted on charges of molesting a 4 year old girl.
    (USA TODAY, March 24, 1994)

barbara mor

the blue rental

oasis 2

Dona Mona a mythical person who lives in CalleReina behind
the tacqueria next to the alley that leads to the electrical power
station beyond which trains rattle night&day on nervous
tracks that make earth a junkie. her shack(xacalli)invisible
among many,a tiny garden inside adobe walls rusted grillwork
enclosing dependent on the days chemicals PeruvianAndes
Brazilian jungle the shitty barrio where one lives&dies simply
whitewashed bone w/one red geranium in her eyesocket the air
is green cockroach sweat a reign of splendor behind the retinas
daily
     en su casa,she is occupied. windows boarded up except
one door nice slants of yellow heat thru pine slats no shadows
no cooking or eating either,no running water (there is a pump
outside if a dog comes to drink it lives but humans die)she
busies herself in serious ways,roaches&scorpions inhabit the
walls 1000 years for a reason stink&poison like otras mujeres
weave blankets&spider webs around their dark corners she
concentrates & the ancient dust enters&departs its fabulous
shapes (people, flowers, tigers pyramids gods) sometimes at

such speed only a blur w/a broom as if sweeping everything
existent awry or her several eyes glow in the dark watching
nothing or she appears sitting straitback cruel wooden chair
in midst of bare sala stares at flickering b/w tv screen hour
upon hour her soaps & religious programs (the brain attracts
hemispheric events) or past midnite she monkeys w/contrast
dials until a black screen w/white fosforos vectors zigzags
flash news & these are transmissions *lloros espectral* from
freeways or other cities, thoughts, nations in other episodes
she is doing bad things on other planets no one knows
anything about zip nada

                    Dona Mona, many personas
as legends say (real advertisements) her lower parts(puta)
wrappt in snakes,or her hair is snakes,or her head is 2
snakes spitting blood from a choppt neck (some holybitch
sacrifice) or bald, as a skeleton shaved & boiled,that
hideous small head wives(once) darned socks on,&
other things *su marido zopenco*   a change of masks,
      clothes or skin, pues, unpleasant but can be done, the
        Toltec art of feathers & jewel embroiderd flesh, or
          flayed girls & boys in their prettiest moments being
         simpatico w/the agonies of calendars,dates sweaty
           synchronies of Crazed power & she also knows the
         gods lose their bowels straining each day one more
        impossible day for who else cleans it up ,sulfurous
      diarrhea & vomitus of gods & blood clots & splatterd
      estomagos (menstrual blood no problem,as it gushes
        from all hearts,white lava from our breasts)
she is also cat piss

Dona Mona walks along as bent vieja the bundle on her
back (aluminum cans pincushions peyote buttons glasseyes
dropped more frequently than one would think de paso
cigarette butts broken rosaries needles spit pickt locks&
scabs butterfly footsteps) beautiful bottle novae that make
each pathway a cathedral window a drunks explosion &/
or both & end of sidewalk & blah la end of lament

Dona Mona assumes this walk of power to do her grocery
shopping she buys nothing but enjoys the ambience of
moving as one of them among the mortalities

the blue rental

Dona Mona I dont know her she is one of those it is best to
see in yr dark alleys & keep on moving

each a.m. her daughters rise & go to the Wal.it is a long
walk over broken pavement boring dust cement no cement
one wears combat boots one sandals one Nike knockoffs a
desert bulldozed grows strange things,reptile creosote&dirt
ambitions what they dreamed uprooted (the dream does not
end thereby) the sisters pass cenozoid rubble,mercados
zapaterias panaderias extinct destinations,big horny toads
crouchd on warpd boards&adobe stumps,gas station w/cacti
between 2 pumps nothing else grows no business here a
great pile of trash the Temple of Garbage,el pueblos
secrets&mysteries old socks underwear tincans mattresses
chewinggum wrappers & virgin brassieres a Pyramid of
sacred items y otras cosas, las hermanas make signs of
personal recognition,there is the broken radio there is the
fatal gun, cholla spines snaggd w/historic debris, xmas
ribbon cassette tapes condoms the wind god tosses small
things around on his way out here & there a marigold
grows from a discarded body part,other mutations also
,freak creatures,bioflorafauna scrabbling & entwining the
nostalgic heap 3headed rats prehensile scorpions motile
ocotillo w/neon eyes all will be happy to feed on toxins,
crap & vast radiations & lots of leaked blood if history is
predictable,all night all day the Pyramid glows in a dark
which probably no ojos have noticed

the daughters Capilla, Flora y Pinche Malinche (o Tres
Parcas as they are known in some neighborhoods) algunas
veces mock,sometimes replay their past glories, e.g. Xingu
jungle eponymous Amazons copulate golden phalluses
up river from where hot chilis on bare pezones made us
fly,Tenochtitlan the Place of the Cactus Fruit,nopal heart
red as cunts our green flesh inherits,this walk of distance
to where Sonora desert dreams to exist one day,a brown
person stops & bows to you,little mescal toci of rocks
peyotl who grows only in this Dead Place,Mictlan of
course,life is a mixt bag the sisters drink Pepsi w/coke as

barbara mor

they walk,toss stupid gossip y blasfemias into the litter,it
goes on & on a heap of existential junk,anaconda skin
umbilicus tampons of lost civilizations they recognize
their family contributions to the stinking pile,obsidian
scissors & jade cigarette lighters,discarded tubes of black
mouth paint lavished upon insatiable earth goddesses
speaking of Dona Mona,her skinny blue dog rummagd the
Serpent Temple of abandoned birds,snakes&wild perritos
akaTeotihuacan,Xolotls HotDogs yCerveza,he disappeared
looking for her boys BunchoyCruncho the horrible workers
mysteriously lost in some parking lot not far from here
los pendejos locos

her daughters not exactly derived from marriage they belong
to that race of beings who losing a tail, grow it back but
never lose nostalgia for the original

they arrive at theWal.aTemple,ritual site of sorts, castle
of Things surrounded by asphalt moat w/dormant cars &
nonindigenous shrubbery,dark green rubbery bushes no
spikes or flores(colores)no discernible regional properties
locate consumers where they are 100s 1000s diurnally
pass thru this sole portal exceptional in its nonentity
considering beneath cement the bodies bound in sisal
rope foetal position enough raw blood poured out to
guarantee commercial success the grayhair greeter does
not reveal that you are all *ixiptlas*
                              they enter backdoor far
down,around monolith in the rear a forbidden entrance
marked EXT they are not "workers" but "extensions"
(ext) swipe ID cards (age nombre horas wages sex debt
destiny planet) como se dice yr life other creatures (exts)
(w/frequent turnover) enter also but do not glow in the
dark as las hermanas,swipe identity,don corporate smock
bluson azul or blue apron that makes them uniform,lock
lockers & begin,woman&man,what jobs become them
before they exuent or grow old die in situ,ID badges on
sunken chests or bosoms swollen w/unrealized romance
bitter denial as if cattlebrands on their foreheads,Las
Parcas of course are not human,their names also glow

in the dark
            Capilla does checkstand,Flora restrooms &
garden,Pinche Malinche womens lingerie (gloves bolsas
belts scarves stockings perfumes & red satin underwear)
under their uniforms their bodies smeared & creamed
w/poison to remain spirits,*Yamuricuma*
Flora in garden & bathroom maintenance grows seeds
in fertilizer no one the wiser & the toilets sing to the
blooms & leaves in a cyclical way that biomedicinally
satisfies her long attentions
Pinche Malinche chooses her face before dressingroom
mirrors as if personas hung on hangers, refers to flayed
ones as superior to cosmetics & facelifts but she(her tits
better than her thoughts)known to lie,red satin lipstick &
bloodred fingernails & cutglass bottles of CelestialPrincess
parfume she uses personally but warns others against it,
pues, somos mujeres poderosas
Capilla at beginning of her shift she wears a smile each
hour ticks the skin grows taut & more taut pulls the
grin back into her ears & the white yellow & broken
teeth are not especially attractive
                        consumers who love bargains
in their swarm of wallets & packages leaking a little
red fluid,or pinkish or chlorophyll or exhausted semen
,soft creatures pushing empty carritos into looming
aisles that will make them full (Flora feels viney things
intruding corporate orifices Malinche observes how
maggots rush to lunch Capilla,not sentimental,counts
$s perhour no pissbreaks no smokes)they put their hands
on wonders of earth,shelves boxes plastoid appliances
&home decor incessant objects alive in fluorescent air
that also renders living things unreal   here are toys
tools glass&clocks canned beans canned tuna chips &
chewingguminallflavors papel higienico(48 rollos
dobles) waterbottles filled w/worm piss, mothers tears
& milky soma computerized coffeemakers toothbrushes
vibrators(the stolid peasants dream they are urban &
lean, they are not)their children run to games,Aztec &
Mayan action figures,warriors goddesses snake priests
&skull racks,ChacMool reclined w/purple jelly hearts in
his little bellydish   not to be outdone Jesus&Satan of

Revelations videobox,St John up to his neck in Blood of
Losers,like Angels believers explode & fuse apocalyptic
bodyparts (little factory girls earn Chinese pennies per
week assembling xtian crosses stigmata & swords,$17.95
retail)Princess dolls, Virgins succubi &burnt witches
monsters of LakeVostok,melting awake globes swirld
w/dinosaurs &quetzals in nostalgic snow,& frozen
mammoth w/undigested bites of appleblossom in their
tripas *were they really so small? are we so big?* O!
cheap oriental imports poison smiley faces who speak
oink oink honk honk a la muerte,gabacho! cliticlac!
down from Mt Chimberazo ecuadorial avalanches pour
ash&soap&oil our civilizations our cavernous interiors
yawn,smog ozone CO2 deranged plantgrowth Bonsai!
onestopshop eschatology *tianquizpan tlayacaque* walk
amid us, market guardians banging huacos & drums
falta de respeto,nobody hears them   empty&emptied
esposas shopt in auras of memories so lulled by matchd
towels washcloths &bathrobes they do not cognate years
katuns baktuns passing while they browse & finger P.
Malinches red satin fantasies o Floras hyenas&vultures
&earthworms chew&vacuum&slime their putrid organs
Siempre Barato! Siempre Mezquino!! Monkey Donuts!!!
next to Capillas checkout bookrack the bestselling Raptor
series by some PeruvianMexican he spells it his way on
the cover large birds descend to pick off naked ascending
creatures but the clothd horizontal soft creatures buying
these books do not seem to fear their destinies surely do
not care who makes them change or records their deb(i)t
or marks their doomsday in the invisible calendar do not
care who passes thru them that makes a change o look!
its time! the little baby smiley face who squeaks *pee pee
oink oink honk honk* the 5th Sun going out of business
sale commences in the basement of the mind where the
gods shop lightbulbs&darkness in the Nahuatl phrase
pay w/yr guts

        after being dead 4 years our warriors return as
hummingbirds&butterflies of course it is their flowery
nature(penises dipt in nectar etc)belonging to daylight,

the blue rental

massacres of theSun
                        females,por otro lado,enter night
as their element &remain,become obsidian easily, girls
after Death go crazy thus the Celestial Princesses don
serious regalia & prepare for work(on certain unlucky
days & on the last day)black mirrors on knees &elbows
,claws & fangs &clacking labia,lava of their veins coold
rapidly &glinting out their eyeballs *Ilhuica cihuapipiltin*
they erupt on highways,at crossroads,traffic stops,each
intersection whore teeth staind red & chicle smacking
wet castanets in their nasty mouths(on 5 unlucky days or
at the end of the world) bochorno sultry breezes from a
desert already drunk the Western sky falls,meanwhile
humble clerks in such positions to devour the world at
the worlds end,swarm & stride & slaughter under their
snakeskirts hang down obscenely violet tongues,thick
knives,hyena clitori   P.Malinche,w/hideous hair &
        bare breasts(her tits better than her thoughts)grabs &
        twists little children into gerbils,mice,feral Disney
        animations carnivorous upon their parents *chinga!*
    & here the DevilWomen monsters of reality ript like
    a curtain,as they say,this fatal twilight hour when sky
    collapses,*Tzitzimime* step thru the wound to devour
    whatever runs what screams,Flora sings their hungry
    flowers,blooms as earth is swallowd her total throat,in
downtown motels,teatros,cafes final images suctiond
    into huge magenta cunt,most monstruo of all Capilla &
    the skinny bitches *Tetzuahcihua* from the mezzanine
    of heaven,women w/no flesh,no pity only bones their
    job to devour all people at the end of the world,tho
    nothing tastes very good anymore they slice & cut w/
surgical fingernails or sprouting serpents &electrodes
    from their heads like chia pets they who as *obreras
    eternas* are in such positions in such ways they are in
    time to eat us at worlds end

so one day there is no Sun
so one day the Sun does not rise, okay

Road of Xibalba Black Road,cunt of our milky galaxy(end

of LongCount,5th Sun 4th Earth)the final trip: *xibalba be*
underworld way she walks forward questioning CAMINAR
PREGUNTO   25,800 years una y otra vez the obscure
procession   a darkness intentional,thick dingy shards&
clots of greasd air corpuscular in the extreme of lungs&last
mucopurulent spasms the dirt upheaves & hearts from
their seismic bodies   so she leaves her abode & walking
the final time perhaps that is when daylight disappears she
walks thru dirty dark w/lizard eyes fixd on theWal she
does not care to put on shawl or jewelry etc does not wear
the old dress worn until it is 3 threads &fell off or even
sweatshirt & pants she does business in in fact she walks
naked pues que nadie can see her cuerpo covered w/snake
scales & increasingly morpht as she goes into a black pelt
or very erotic jaguar in huaraches over the noninhabitual
streets
    (American roads paved w/Venezuelan oil,tar,asphalt
deinos Saurischia Ornithischia driven fromOrinoco basin)
along LaFrontera border which is 18ft tall concrete&steel
toppt razorwire &embedded glass w/terminal cicadas
bats rattlers w/white eyes cataracting down the stone a
memory squeezed so hard it can weep she talks to earth
(a criminal activity)listens to earth *peyote mescal hongo*
opio along w/her black footprints of one who is never
seen,black pus of laughter   walks to Wal where gringos
sell each other air&sex&time&matter 13 lunations pass
thru her eyesockets like jelly thru water as men perform
theSuns glory,so females extract surrender moche brujas
todas comadronas who help doomed *entes* die,Totomac
12OldWomen who own the soil,sweep warriors&kings
toMictlan w/brooms dript w/blood,so elSol his final day
theBlackHole sucks him in & his eyes roll back to 0000
    : Time to teach sun how to eat worms & die

Dona Mona at theWal *perpendicular y total* ,wall of
background stars,nightUniversetime,completeinventory&
weight ofThought 14 degrees tiltPlane ofEcliptic alignd w/
intersects su hoyo *you&me,senor* Void&*gravedad*,a wall
of skulls who smile,copal smoke exudes their nostrils *you*
have expended much breath to get here (aMexica greeting)
not at all

the blue rental

el hado ruinoso wall of bulletholes gritos puke
blueballpoint notes to Mary&Jesus,bad photos nombres of
the dead all thats left Junk derived from dull flesh,war
plunder markets 7/11 cigarettes motoroil natures replication
of species as even cockroaches dream of rosas&true love,or
maybe not What counts isTime,timing is everything sd
theWitch when there are so many of them they cease to
seem personal except perhaps to their mothers but then
do insects have feelings? bloodsmear & advertisements,
hammerd nails of rhetorical questions,the selfhypnosis of
gods everywhere they go el paraiso into a dump,mirage
del cielo now rusted cars now stupid dust
DonaMona stands in emptiness & talks to It,Entropy,the
parking lot coldbeer toad secretions those lost hijos,
Plata y Plomo,circling the drain of Westerncivilization
contrario a las manecillas del reloj
                              she does her part,
teotleco,They return,Tezcatlipoca at the beginning,who
stitchd dogheads to dogbutts to make our first ancestors
madre&padre mom&pop that forkdTongue snake,that
sexy blackcat,nakedly strolls toTollan paintd headtofoot
Green,a salesman of GREEN PAINT *ha!* a mirror on one
foot(I am),back of his head(yr stupid face)a black wind
everywhere,rain of black knives   & the girls,busy
elsewhere,check out the consumers of breath,se despiden
goodbuy goodbye morir to die heaping stuff upon stuff
in collapsing biospheres the air suckd out into bigger
seers,wall of skulls who only smile(perfect teeth& no
eyes selling nada anymore)when they look in yr eyes&
say this humanos you will laugh some say you get yr
just desserts to us it is just dessert ha ha

*from such minute perspectiveUniversecomplex&full as
from a god or rich man or myself,me i abhor aVacuum
that is why you are abhorrent yr empty cartons&boxes
of crap,every square inch must be filled,even fleas are
conscious from their sweat holy tears,itz ,waters of
prognostication violet killer sap&translucid fluid,as
ch'ulel Mayan soulstuff,exploded in blood,we conjure
tzak our work Today & the ch'u who enjoy us*
                              thus DonaMona

hallucinates colors,spews on Wal FastGreenBrilliantBlue
QuinolineYellowAmaranthSunsetYellow red red red
everywhere isIndigoCarmine sprayd between her teeth&
other lethal food properties w/marvellous nombres on
theWal 50,000 years of graffiti promo for the emerging
brain,shit splashd w/out permission many walls magic
squares hexagrams hieroglyphs bits of blown heads she
envisions a black mushroom cloud & it happens
intonan intota tlaltecuhtli tonatiuh "for our mother &
our father,the earth&the sun
    she does her part of an old chocho *old woman of*
itching buttocks Madre de losTodos,slut,landlady of
worms,patrona tacono,curses everything sur norte
oriente occidente el accidente plays no favorites all my
   children maldito&maldito&maldito:binary numbers
:Ch'uey&Fooey(FuHi,1stEmperor,Chinese got here
first)(how do men do this bang their brains ofWhat they
make&demandThis is Law the ultimate boundary this
isGod not me o yes! i forget theWal is my cunt let me in
  let me in! hombresymujeres who bear them are driving
nature crazy senor &to beBornAgain from elDioVaron
requires think about it a very small head *[una cabeza*
   muy menudo])
                  she does her part:
you fuckt it up you fuckt it up again you stupid bingos!!
she could scream that she screams that inside her head
but in reality she is silent her daughters busy elsewhere
(&w/her footprints,One who is never seen,prick fucking
everything,delicious joy)she busies her invisible body
sweeping up sudden eons of blood,of kings&warriors&
salesmen&shoppers&todos otros w/a relentless
broom

hypatia

it is clear here in the copy place where we(may) reproduce
ourselves in calm
it is clear here in the copy place where we reproduce our
selves in calm

- how you select the correct alignments (8"9"11") the lid
  is down
  check darkness-number-size depress copy button
  and the brilliant light passes over
- and the brilliant light passes over   many times,specify
  or once only,the repeat above each time: solo pass,light
  repeat above

shells waves replicating patterns   scoop her flesh mind time
into the future as the sea (clone)

i have no memory then of anything but black line emerging
graph on white space no memory(need fear purpose physical
discomfort)but the graph emergent of white with black with

rough etched texture or precise ink hieroglyphs perfections of
all copies

- i taught mathematics astronomy philosophy (clone)
- and how they scooped with lovely large shells the shape of
  oceans burning thighs of the sea

i taught astronomy in Alexandria, 4th-5th c. of their time
also algebra, geometry and hydrology i specialized in
conic sections, uses of the astrolabe, Neoplatonic sciences
my father Theon, Orphic scholar, professor of pagan religion
magic astrology dream divination, above all Astronomy
condemned by Christians among the "black arts" I,like Theon
renowned for eloquence, brilliance, astute wit, encircled
by many students   a woman by nature honored before
the victory of other minds

-think a style of Erosion   Erasure -

put it down and then begin to erase it gradually and
allow it to erode
                rotten places   crumbled interior brick walls where
a room of jewels emerges red vines
            or the erosion of Gargoyles

Notre Dame cathedral resculpted the gargoyles eroded by
rain in our throats
a plastoid sealant on the (stained) windows of Chartres
protect from Time,pollution but the luminous the
luminous is gone

-and how they scooped with clean female shells the pain
of oceans the mind of the sea

presumed to teach men   not remarkable,teachers of men
in all things my sex bore the Mind in a dark cave
which is the skull the womb & great night   this they found

intolerable,ruled by doctrine of a vile and unconscious
Nature. "holy" they called themselves,not from Cosmos but
from a Book
-earth is flat the Universe squat like a tabernacle
-science is Evil,submission a Virtue
-disease fear ignorance are Mysteries
-a woman teaching men is Sin
such was their dogma   some religion dript like poison froth
from the mouths of madmen,stunningly empowered,the most
prurient&mean among them,to great heights:bishops archbishops
popes "Saints"
who lust for nothing real   a womans nakedness helpless some
bird stripped of feathers a whimpering dog   unlike cruel
Rome,which sought public amusement in wounds of strong men,
these "holy men" fly to heaven on womens screams,Christs
wounds are vulvas,my raped legs spread as bloody wings
i did not scream

-Cyril,the Instigator,Bishop of Alexandria,despised among
us as misogynist, Paulist, ambitious liar (but
does not one term include the others)desired mathematicians
be torn by beasts or burned alive: he became with my death
therefore a virulently potent man in the region,and then
of course a Saint
)after my death,that is: his business did quite well
after my death he said I was alive and living in Athens

a womans hand the adjacent copier white flutterd intrusion
of ghosts from a sidestreet into her eyes swiftly mutely she
reproduces her duties are they memories assignments collations
they are paper.some flesh with signs on it,they scratch
directions on you map yr skin as to where you will be disposed
of. or the names of all the schools the cries the books of
oceanography that will proceed from you   the floating pieces
her final paper flutters to the floor and she retrieves it
she never looks to one side or another this is her lifes work

my murder on the other hand ends Platonic teaching in
Alexandria,throughout the Roman Empire every item of

intelligence consigned to Fire : mss & books,the Library razed,
utterly pillaged the great School of Philosophy – poetry music
medicine geology geometry astronomy calculus -- the sacred
learning of the known world *which proved them wrong.* a
rabid religion must attack the Earth: thought art exstasis
denied them, fanatic thugs destroy all evidence they exist
reduced to wasteland the ancient world as they would do
to (my) flesh
when there was little left to rip insult & burn,they turned to
my fame.   when that was gone   they turned to the future.

i am told they succeeded

        a strange face strange hair eyes of mirror seafoam
greengray,black as history gazes back &knows then forgets
she might be a woman of genius abandoned husband and/or
children to write in a bare room desperate fictions or construct
philosophies of our disappearance her cause is hopeless
on her back inventing God on my knees scrubbing cloister
floors which she entered to study algebra or catalog
poetry of asylums,her ink personal blood stealthily extracted
womans work as daily excrement is womens work
staring into washtubs toilets abattoirs bowels of diapers&
hospital sheets the Void men make a philosophy of
daily female practice scouring foul tenets pretend to heal
war poverty lust conduct economies of scale i count out
toothpicks string bouillon cubes she became an old woman
selling old spoons in a doorway with no teeth,or in some
battlefield ditch or brothel she was once beautiful or brave but
nameless nothing survives but anonymous bodies struggled
to achieve Entelechy inside one bare room one day walked
out walked into a bus walked into a lake died of absence

        we rode in a chariot which is a final imagination
(copy)   the young man with me my student Synesius
of Cyrene if a lover that ended abruptly as the first shell
scooped me out

"To be short, certain heady & rash cockbrains whose guide

& captain was Peter, a reader of that Church, watched the
woman coming home from some place or other" wrote
Socrates Scholasticus, 5th c. Christian historian "they pull her
out of her chariot: they had her unto the Church called
Caesarium: they stripped her stark naked; they raze the
skin & rend the flesh of her body with sharp shells, until
the breath departed out of her body: they quarter her body:
they bring her quarters unto a place called Cinaron and
burn them to ashes."

the Parabolans, Cyrils Guard who served as Church enforcers
a gang of thugs who spread rumors of my "witchcraft" &
"black magic," instigated by Peter the Reader, church lector
perhaps clergyman "a perfect believer in all respects in
Jesus Christ"
who did not want me read but RED all my blood documented
[all is Text]
"the [last] pagan woman" murdered by "a multitude of believers
in God" [John of Nikiu] also called "beasts" [Damascius]

naked,dragged into their church,sliced & butcherd with "broken
bits of pottery" and/or "sharp oyster shells" Or, I was dragged
naked thru streets until dead. Or, I was torn to pieces "….and
her body shamefully treated parts of it scattered all over
the city"

   Synesius saved himself by professing to be a Christian
-and later became bishop of Ptolemais

my death occurred during Lent, March 415AD, I was 40,45,60
or some age. Investigation of my murder repeatedly postponed
for "lack of witnesses." Eventually Cyril proclaimed it
hadnt happened
Cyril thus "destroyed the last remnant of idolatry in the city"

And Alexandria was no longer troubled by philosophers.
                              Bertrand Russell,1945   [copy]

i am making copies of knowledge
the straw lit,then kindling then large branches & the pyre

107

flames up becomes her body & all flesh for one moment as
sweating wax suggests the requisite mortality   it is all
a business so much for the judge scribe torturer so much
straw bedding etc days weeks in a cell what she eats bread
meat salt fish,wine for the guards,the woman who comes to
shave her (head armpits legs pubis devils live in our hair)
the laborer who cuts the wood those who search her house
for magic powders cost of paper to record the trial (11 leaves
approx +ink)cost of transport to trial & the pyre,cost of
wood,wagon plus 2 judges w/charrd lump to a grave pit,her
property confiscate by Church & State children disinherit
present the bill to the corpse   a woman sometimes old
often young,wife or virgin strippt exorcised depilated
tortured several days,weeks (centuries of this)undergone
w/priests blessing the instruments sadistic tools applied to
quiverous flesh w/a kiss after this burning is incidental
all a business *pan et circensus* a banquet goes on the bill
lawyers physicians mayors clergy &soldiers feast&drink
copiously,men larded by stench of their salvation,crowds
fill towns,innkeepers &taverners prosper it is a major
industry called eating pain,scooping out food &eating
great agony of bodies denied the soul lives (they say) it is
all about the disembodied soul
    -this woman gets her ComeUppance
    -thinks shes so damn smart
    -a God who can lower the mighty presume to teach men
     abomination,beat her to her knees & grovel upside cocky head
     w/Gods big cock open her mouth to scream
    -utter philosophy her oral poetry i'll give her oral
    -jism Up Her Ass w/some silence
    -haw haw haw
    -shut her mouth
    -what we could do to them all,given the Time
    -slice out big pieces of bitch brain stick it on a sharp stick
     roast it in the fire like marshmallows
    -the Length of Gods private member up her bitch Vagina
     shovit all the way to the *dura mater*,w/stifled screams
    -call it History
    -call it Law
    -call it World
    -haw haw   haw haw

the blue rental

her nervous compulsion at the machine,manacled by
technology her hands process occult letters & our tidal
eyes,papers documents trial records which become the
scientific method *as if her anatomy still dissected by a*
burning light [F.Bacon, Aphorism124], his Inquiry of secret
places as basilisks & newts jump from boiling womb, &
lucrative metals,*her diamonds & natives & raw lands i give*
unto you, a preponderance of "witch marks" occur inside the
labia majora which he inspects for its great wealth,Iron or
gold extract'd or new Laws of physiks Always the objective
man enters Caves,seas & sexual venues w/eye to Profit, &Time
born from such Plunder,*Nature on the rack* etc joints, levers
sulfurs & engines of Her perverse dreams in our hands
not monsters but Power,as maggot,marrow &menstruous hair
become fish&snakes from fish&snakes "squeezed&molded"
cum Coin & property,Her slime accrues his Mind via Alchemy
All Matter mechanized (dumb) or Evil (female) she
must not read Books but be Open'd as a Book,scann'd
as woodcuts & color'd plates show ladders pulleys & platforms
erected into herInnerSelf already wounded by Definition,he
performs "a very diligent dissection & anatomy of the World"
over & over upon her dead body the machiney rolls,she
does not scream

Silence is the kosmos of women   Sophokles,5th c. bce
(Sophokles who burned in the same flame as Hypatia

the copies of herself   office memos birth &death files
tv scripts novel passages *which are not her* temporal
bodies reflected in glass 9 to 5 contract w/money she
strangely performs then disappears to motel sleep,cemetery
apt shared w/a cat the humming efficiency of ancient
landscapes *we were bees in Ephesus workers in honey our*
beating urgencies our Kosmos our good order build the
hallucination of honey a female machine that is broken the
druidic codes love potions of Thrace documents of buzzing
epiphanies they must not read .or receding streets into
suburbs of located normality there is a bank there is a

church there is a school there is a life *once oracle once*
Delphi once pythoness of the world her body busy & lost
watching thru glass children in plastic pools wives&husbands
joined in squat marriage over toiletbowl&insurancepapers
the Female clitoris qua ontologic pleasure grows larger a
male organ *close lips suture scrotum* the phallus a clitoris
both magnified & distanced via the entertainment of Risk,a
soap opera now sad appendages of mayonnaise & backyard
barbecue attempt normalcy squat as in original cave over
newly discovered fire,drip blood & grease
(a student, young & ideational,professed Love,i
removed my menstrual bandage & dangled it before his
horrific eyes, Sir do you love this? I thought not
the male is weak.   the fastidious sex thus becomes
a Tyrant. & i remain a Virgin

return to mechanical reproduction   attempt paraphrase
a woman at the next copier moves in dream,in her head a
lighted room she enters but does not know how,her name,or
what for
   obedient ovulations = family breeding
   advanced thought   = the bird flies,wings artificially alive
                                        as beating electrons of no air
   factories of men   = organs of women
a ring on her finger,around her neck aura of seizure
in the event of historic amnesia memory retrieval as a disease
all institutions are erasers they rub her flesh blank
she does not seem to think her work occurs elsewhere
& other times
and every room lights up,she enters, radiant with light but
the other rooms forgotten she doesn't know she exists (ever)
otherwise/in them   bereft ovulations   1600 years
datum of women

"The universal social pressure upon all women to be all
   alike, and do all the same things, and to be content with
   identical restrictions, has resulted not only in terrible
   suffering in the lives of exceptional women, but also in the
   loss of unmeasured feminine values in special gifts. The

the blue rental

Drama of the Woman of Genius has so often been a
tragedy of misshapen & perverted power."
Anna Spencer, Womens Share in Social Culture,1913

"Sexually awakened women, affirmed & recognized as such,
would mean the complete collapse of the authoritarian ideology."
Wilhelm Reich, The Mass Psychology of Fascism,1933

"Christianity desires to dominate *beasts of prey*; its means
for doing so is to make them *sick*."
Friedrich Nietzsche, The Anti-Christ,1888

among crowds of,nicely dressed who are normal(are tame)
w/inside a beast beast plugged umbilical to machine machine
to industry industry to a Corpse,the terminus God or planet
inside walls emitting on/off messages   Monday 10a.m.
9th & A Spring 21st c. *the destination of Earth is*,Now
Is Money male&female equal in pursuit of,All Is Commodity
resurrect that Sexy beast! sell you buy me digital flatline as
empty happy efficient clean automaton of money do not
struggle question sweat sufficient pain to be otherwise,dots
pulsed thru eyes on way to entropy *i recur as Hypatia*
among sick animals   avoidIntonation,do not scream

therefore,they are clones cognizant of monitored 24/7
computer surveillance worksite public toilet cellphone
mall shopping fucking in cars asleep in backyards dying
in libraries some go in disguise carry extra 15-20 pounds
attach curly wig grow mustache wear sunglasses the ones
in suit tie &cleavage all on elevators all smell the same
to disappear in crowds to be unknown as if dead not there
blur on video screen too identical of job & dream to
be identified by name   10:32 70F 21C   World Ends
in 5 Minutes HaveNiceDay   Bank US

               ... ...

her hands,she,i   frequently the water like a skin becomes
us,or we become whatever the woman assigned by,adrift
as seaweed in this element the clinging pieces fleshly salt

glue Desire "a viscous fingering" describes the lust of,flow
& sticking of matter reaches Life as "growth by repeating
pattern" bacteria coral fire mountains plague lung &
cloud each aspect of a Body i secrete,try on, repeat,move
on "....first order models of rivers, watersheds, botanical
trees, & human vascular systems" fractaling ion to ion
asDesire replicates everywhere Itself,expanding & Alone
in Egypt each year Sirius ascendent w/the Sun,as our
year begins our great star conjunct w/a star, they climb
& everything is reborn in generous thick overflow of a
river,midsummer DogStar &Hawk pulled into blue skylap
of their mother Nut   as Ptolemy's Tetrabiblios in
Alexandria taught us & my father Theon,,e.g. "On Signs
& the Examinations of Birds & the Croaking of Ravens"
Sirius rises w/Horus & great Nile ejaculates,fields lush
in spermy heat,womens bellies ignite by stars All Things
conjoind in Desire,as we observd,flow &adhesion of Vital
Lust,that great burst from which flung out as *effluvia*
all the fiery & planetary bodies,first Orgasm populating
Void w/mysteries of Thought,thought w/mysteries of Objects
objects w/mysteries of Desire galaxies worlds continents
wind over ocean ocean over rock blood sweat semen tears
all Salt all sacred equally flung wet cells into repeating
of this Time that is Original
                              Diakosmos,from *potentia*
a Universe, jewels & drama upon nakedness She may
wear Generations of amusement then suddenly in boredom
rip them off,plunge into Darkness to dream the next world
so Pythagoras & Stoics Parmenides & Plato observers
of Eclipse,as the Saros each 18.64 years Sun crossed by
Moon in the Cold Solstice,this could be the end of the
world oceans rivers lymph & milk pulled heavily into
one terrible place of the Sky,tides of massacres &nameless
animals drownd&rotting,awful chokes &eyeballs bulged
w/last visions "scientists look for things that obey laws,
they do not look for things that don't obey laws" but
all things follow law,it is not obedience but Desire,a
tropism as Chaos to numbers Eros to words & then the
great reversal as she devours Herself in a tedium or
rage to forget,begin again. they forget wild law,rise &
fall of a phallus,Arousal of caged beasts,slaves eating

masters "once every 175 years conjunction of 2 outer
planets" once every 1000 minutes collision of meteors &
black spirals

oceanic,time & foam & there appear miraculous my
hands. we demonstrate all erotic body parts but it is
these hands that do things to you: button yr coat,point
a finger, wind clocks & cut the thread *shave you head
to foot preparatory to salacious torture* bloody
like prayer $50 manicure magazine thighs & deadly
perfume,these appendages are th'advertised scythes of
Doom chop chop *how do you like yr women* wrapt
in cellophane & rayon,defurred & detongued, i move
among men easily,clottd fingernails scratching out my
own brains the cosmetic words are *free* & *lost* a Logos
of pricetag,a portent of endless scream   i am the
corporate head of important Bodies,or her victims,or
lawyers on both sides of her Trial,or i could care less
what happens to her i wash my hands in piss water
these fingers are mythic&bored or i care so much for
everything i can't breathe,i am always weeping i am
always smiling on camera while things explode &all
this is photogenic,keep busy in common sink,female
gelatinous gestures that once gods extrude a world,*the
more forced flow the more spread* increasing desperate
odds,we are free & lost together this gluey confusion
is profitable,my angles in her chemicals,my face
dissolved in all mirrors   until   my dears,it is Time
she says to Reverse,slimemold &Fate periodically
as the Tides,change yr Mind & hands appear thick
as a ship made of dead witchs' cuticles,very expensive
primeval claws scratching at yr bones i look down they
could be mine,gnarld versatile stumps,brass knuckles,
or lovely hands of Fate which can be lovely,*strange
attractors*

hypatia must read newspapers study events w/scissors
select cut out photos,headlines disasters dates one
murder one rape one broken mind per second per hour
one seduction one kiss one slit or strangled throat or
bullet file these,level upon level in sediments of an

infinitely deep time of infinitestimal accumulations as
"growth by aggregation" a world of physics,cries,facts
is built up,atom into subject into universe as one
brick upon brick composes a solid wall & then blood
splatters on it & shriek of red dots decoded has also
a pattern,a nova   as hypatia observed the night sky
beyond numbers or miniscule thought variations,how
the world from one cell becomes this   massacre
war famine repeat repeat rich poor fat starve ugly
beautiful repeat try to change(erase) atrocity revolt
return to original repeat talk talk break break repeat
repeat(women are free to partake of all this women
are lost inside bags of weeping)one burned book one
beaten virgin one mans holy war upon one woman
pornography hagiography calligraphy of my moving
finger on my brain wall monotonous (kill the woman
who studies history the repetition is so obvious this
redundance 200 million sperm per shot repeat repeat) &
she abides it again & again abets it as if *the human
condition* & every wound becomes a religion becomes
a prison becomes an industry that makes new wounds
bigger nastier more profitable repeat repeat &my
sex colludes w/this desecration of (our)Nature until
it becomes Our Nature

Prague,1994,first commercial tv station postSoviet
world Czech Republic NOVA flowering ideals of
social & cultural life,finagled by "American cosmetics
money"EsteeLauder family taxdodge into tabloid
sex&violence enterprise "meeting public demand"
American women,who could not buy their own tv
station,nor radio,not even a major newspaper in the
best of lives,yet billions of dollars of pretty lipstick
&deodorant&perfume(& vanity & silence)pours
from them into women of neoVictorian "free market"
their capital deficient enslavement to femme wiles&
image paranoias,at cost of Mind cosmetics exist in
this world to decorate corpses,ornament wounds w/
bloodcolor as if historic air kisses them,thus death
goes away daub stench of rot &corruption,fear w/
sweat of flowers,sad exhalation from the slaughtered

petals so you cannot tell the difference a woman hit
black&blue a woman trying desperate to seduce you
rouge raw & lurid global eyeshadow surely if i do
not protest one i will not fight the other,broadcast as
a terminal clown,Advertisement for Do It Again(or
she cowers inside a bag,a corpse or a corpse,you
choose,God's whore or Market whore,not the oldest
profession the oldest profession is Man

kosmos: order, a universe *kosmetos*: well-ordered
kosmein: to arrange *kosmetikos*: skilled in arranging

clouds of exhaled gods squat on a city,Pharos is not
in the harbor,nothing breathes sewers&surrogate life
under some stale idea this is the weather report
       humanity,bred to hate itself 2000 years reaches a
logical conclusion Let it end,a prophecy of old men fixd
as virus on itsHost,fed on reproduction grown fat ticks
on genitals gorged w/misery the home the family the
heaven which never existed,the safe bed far away from
war,it never was the Holy which are heretics then products
then wealth then weapons hammer the mind never think
never dream never become except perversion,a religion
of old mens wetdreams plagueInquisitionlaying of tick
eggs in yr eyes,tuberculosis of sooty air,firebombs
mustardgas he breathes into you like soul,millennia of
autoViolence as yr Way to Glory,the Pious God the
Righteous Godthe God of BloodMoney multiplication
of a bad dream,some Hatred called religion &theEnd
of everything crazed young men ejaculate napalm
uranium anthrax into white black red yellow vaginas of
all colors we are in the mob of resentment now,who
betray themselves to be PureLies,what lives beyond
mass suicide the good,the good old boys &good wives
chokd on their knees,they laugh haw haw tears fall of
marriage,divorce kitchentable abortions dirty hangers
& biblical fingers into shivering bodies,suffer for the
Lord of SuperiorFlesh,MoralValues which never
existed beyond property beyond fear beyond crowded
little animals together in a dark den as monotonal war
drones over the price of sex the cost of Sex the God

barbara mor

Who Judges Sex punish punished punishment of this
woman for HumanBiology,*which does exist* her
autonomy that evolved HumanMind &it is my mind
they lust to scoop out,Body&Mind my mouth &my
mouth &my mouths SHUT UP

ressentiment sd Nietzsche the morality of slaves not
bodies forced to labor but minds volunteered to "sin"
self-defined as "sinful" to merely Belong,prostrate
before gods not their own *bloom'd miraculous from
eachSpine* but some words,dript ejacula on paper wads
vengeful ink of OldMen(the future not theirs,never
again except as GodsLaw),beg for a masters whip to
simply feel Identity,Being which their overlord forbids
except this chronic shame,spread to every streetcorner
of earth the converted strut the pious cringe "where
every noble morality develops from a triumphant
affirmation of itself,slave morality from the outset says
No to what is 'outside,' what is 'different,' what is
'not itself,' and *this* No is its creative deed. This
inversion of the value-positing eye—this *need* to direct
one's view outward instead of back to oneself—is
of the essence of *ressentiment*: in order to exist,slave
morality always first needs a hostile world" &ghosts
flutter out,from alleys&sudden gusts of paper that
cut,razorthin Godwound: *excise genitals,fuck the
resultant wound* a vile lust displaced to "devils" i.e.
the corpse of my gods good town matrons who
shave&search theBody w/Questions the flesh is by
now undulating in pain i.e. undergoing sufficient
punishment it happens again everything alive blinded
for their eyes,crucified for their lust,ankles wrists
Rings of pain embrace the body the torturers Bridal
Union w/our Flesh,hands jewel'd w/erotic depravities
No,one single jewel,boil of Power to do so,the Penile
Eye w/a black spider shitting on it,shitting & gouts
of blood flying into walls all joints of the body are
now divorced,the torturers spasms of Kiss,the rack,&
holy instruments all my memories of flesh,holy fires
lit inside them remember this is how they salvage
souls an extraction business the heart,the craft the

secrets raked from ash,sold,dealt as lotteries call'd
the NextTime dingy shops of teeth,gold dentures
shoes watches buttons,little toys all in ncat pilcs
remember yr presence more than once theres more
where that came from Haw Haw
since, now, sd Reich, *the core of the energy release*
of the Living has been excluded & ostracized by men
for ages, truth must needs be evaded, too. Truth is
being evaded because it is unbearable & dangerous
to the organism which is incapable of using it.
something vomits on straw they drag me naked to
their church,do it to me in a church some food they
hand to their God a genital cream which only comes
in such dungeons where we scream *it is happening*
again
& the aristocrat says "most people don't find sex
that pure, that deep, that organic…." instead, they
find it "sort of partial & hot & ugly"
& the lover says sex is "better off dirty, damned, even
slavish! than clean & without guilt" because for Him
Guilt constitutes "the existential edge of sex" w/out
which the act is "meaningless"
& the priest says
  "You see, I think sex has always been dangerous.
  In the Middle Ages, before modern medicine or
  contraception, a woman had to love a man, or feel
  huge lust, in order to have intercourse with him,
  because if she got pregnant she could die. Very
  easy to die—something like 1 in 10 women died
  in childbirth. That meant yr lover could be yr
  executioner. Maybe that's the way it was meant
  to be. God's intent."
sex shouldnt be violated he sez take it seriously
in the Middle Ages bereft by biblical Fiat of ancient
knowledge of her body,pagan biology,Egypt burning
at thc stake,forbidden sex a question occurring at the
mercy of celibate Sons of God embracing vengeance
of God on her terrestrial flesh *peccatum originale*
Sin at the Origin of Earthly Life my desire that
shapes Evolution becomes His Curse,& when did
they respect sex *breeding females like cattle* who

thinks his little 20 second squirt of sperm gives him
the right to own Humanity.   that Sex should be
dangerous for the Female,that is, punishable by
Death (her death) to enhance the puny *frisson* of his
engagement,Man pretends to be On Top of It he
needs that little thrill not of his death but of the
Other
cf St Cyril,the kind of men who succeed

"The ONE God and the ONE Son of God: both
products of bitter resentment…."

"….I cannot endure the way they have of rolling up
their eyes to Heaven—"

Piety's orgasm

Fellowship Church in Chicago, 4 week ceremony
for young Christian girls who call themselves
HANDMAIDENS pubescent teens make public
covenant,a Wedding to Marry Jesus they receive a
ring,marry God & vow to remain chaste ("Virgin")
until marriage "i feel God is loving me,has HisHands
over me,i'm protected byHim,He is there as Lord,my
Husband…."says 15 year old Handmaiden her fathers
hands unfold her like a white sheet
keep her tame,as the Incestors say,keep her sweet
& at Purity Balls,young girls in company w/their
fathers pledge abstinence "i won't kiss a boy until i
get married!" says 9 year old,pretty in ballgown,
eat white cake & vows exchanged w/Daddy, first
dance w/Daddy,girls may date Daddy safely he sd.
(funded partly by govnt faithbased initiative $$$$
which mandates no STD or contraceptive info) 90%
of those who make abstinence pledge break it, a
lifetime of erotic Guilt guaranteed

the bodies of young girls w/no protest up for Grabs
bodies of shy antennae,the tongues of birds,pudendas
of little birds throb in waiting for Daddy, or for sale
"the dominion which was liberty to her" he sd

the blue rental

Butterflies are the most sensitive indicator insect.
A mosquito spray is 100 times more powerful than
what it takes to kill an adult butterfly.
Killing mosquitoes is killing the butterflies.
They are disappearing all over the world.

how to move   the leaves in wind,light on retinas
something articulates sky as wingspan hawk brown
translucent as it circles the axle of bones
who sees this is revealed to be a form of vegetable
body transported on stretchers by robot or automatic
wheelchair in the group moving session
reveal all movement suckt from world into the human
mind self-conscious but paralyzed by this
the muscles fail their definitions
at group sessions they talk of motion how to move
once they workshoppd around how to relate & then
disappeared into sanctuaries of virtuous reality & now
dysfunctional body must discuss to recall retrieve
simple motion   even how to speak
even how to blink
learn biomuscular anatomical stepbystep description
of a movement into & out of
a life
the instinct & natural process becomes sclerosis so
determined they are painful hard & full of grief &
all but extinct
they dwell as fossils their names are Flowing Clouds
Running Wind Gallop Fly the Sky
bloom erupt uncurl explode implode the destinies
of forms they live now only in mind & wistfully give
names to this which is always & forever
lost

                    Theon my father,a pagan
scholar,all fathers since policemen or priests. forbid girls
read the Fathers secret knowledge of his fecal libraries
we are inspired by words we realize Art recognize Nature
as our own go out to comprehend jungles speak w/Fire
what we were forbidden,to gaze at the Pit between our

legs & know the Void is not necessarily Hostile – or
Indifferent.

--your father doesn't want you to have those
my mother slid back her bedroom closetdoor,pointed in
silence to a dozen redbound books on the high shelf.
Books of Knowledge,of adventure classic fairytales
folktales legends poems of ancient history mythology
it was 1942,i was 6 it was the only comment she ever
made about my father,a rare visit to their small room
in a small house in a small world in a War
your Father doesn't want you to have those
but i had them   & i had them all

mid20th c. we went surf-fishing below Pt Dume Malibu
not yet Dawn we drank red wine as dark erased,erase
March fog,chill i caught the first fish,another then as
light,warmth came i went to climb rocks,explore the
beach a woman southward running her horse in surf,the
strong ankles of the sea i began climbing up&up,dirt
path,rock to the top of Dume hunched over the ocean
lay down in my jacket,jeans head on arm to sleep,groggy
w/wine. for how long i woke from,a horse push at my
head,woman on his back gazed down "he thought you
were dead" i rose in a full sun,turned to look out,down
to the sea 2 California gray whales coming north from
Baja the larger,lead whale just below as i stood up
it breached heaved over,dived disappeared in a deep
lunge of ocean,then lifted up Rose huge motion slow
Rocket out of the sea straight up,the absolute sun
dazzling him,all the way to the flukes and he hung
there,stopped the world in Wild salute of joy forever
then in another slow time sank down dazzling dazzling
into the sea reappeared far north spouting laughing
rolling as the companion followed,due north home
to breed i turned, woman & horse were gone the
synchronous kiss of the horse,awaking a Dead Woman
the perfect Salute of the whale,the earth & the sea

write it never happened
right it never happened

the blue rental

... ...

All meaning is an Angle – ancient Egypt
Skating comes from the Blade – Elvis Stojko, 20th c.

       the bees angle to the Sun,*Apis*
mellifera beo bhei bion western honeybee describe/
perform light tangent to our Home Cretaceous
fossil, 70-100 million years,Africa into Europe all
hemispheres making flowers pollinating agents,as
small animals&birds bloom everywhere,apples berries
almonds onions citrus&melons sunflowers,following
flowers perhaps we(humans) came,eating Light
geometry geomentry the terrestrialMind angles
to Earth,spine vectors to Sun&Moon,tiny roots of
growing things in darkness know where we are, 97
degrees heat of buzzing bodies the amber hexagons
of the great dance,sweet angle Love that is ancient
honey   *Our treasure lies in the*
beehives of our knowledge. We are perpetually on our
way thither,being by nature winged insects &honey
gatherers of the mind. The only thing that lies close
to our heart is the desire to bring something home to
the hive. – Friedrich Nietzsche, 1887
& then the great reversal,Earths deep octave,grief
the bees are gone   America Poland India Brazil
massive failure of the Hive,disappear billions billions
female Workers leave behind wax packed w/honey,
starving larvae,the helplessQueen,no dead bee bodies
anywhere,silent the Deathly hive   as if good house
wives,crazy hivewives just walk out,leave full
cupboards & refrigerators,meals in the freezer,kids
dying in their beds just walk out the only door &
Disappear

i am making copies of knowledge *Mind is necessary*
to make the world work in the transition from Possibility
to Actuality. John von Neumann 1955 Mathematical
Foundations of Quantum Mechanics *consciousness,*

*site of wave function collapse,where mystery of matter
becomes mystery of mind,*the quantum jump would
be My Mind

mysterious. i can be mysterious

Ptolemy,text of 13 books, Syntaxsis Mathematica the
Mathematical Treatise medieval Arab scholars called
ALHAGEST "the Great Book" my father Theon & I
Hypatia worked on this among our hours,the Sun
rolled around us as if enTranc'd the Bees also as
unobserved Universe is possibilities POTENTIA
nothing lives here but vibration,Chaos & Desire &
Mind by entering makes something happen by mere
observation ACTIVATES a potential & it becomes
Reality,or Quantum thoughtforms buzz around
Discourse of Elemental Mind (events stay in this
dream until I observe,look in,they collapse,combine
or fractal into multievents of multiworlds,& thus
my view collapses Chaos into World,e.g.Newtons
classical Universe,one of many I said. if God was
Newtons Eye,or BenthamsPanopticon IS an Eye,but
not sufficient:only the Eye of a Fly approaches us,a
Holograph ofBeing. Cosmos views itself is lived
expands,collapses in the same Eye it telescopes
microscopes explode,implode the View of Itself
into Itself the fractur'd eye ofInsect orBeeWing
angling,or cells of Thought abandoned in her Last
Flight

worked to death, the beekeeper said. fetching pollen,
lovemating flowers,spewing honey it was all an
ecstasy for them,all in a days work their ecstatic
Dance,& thence the world we know of animals,fruits
vegetables,eroticFlowers, turned into an Industry,
shipped in cold trucks,region to region season to
season,factory workers chain'd to the clock,man's
MoneyTime which has no mercy,never rests,they
lose their sense of direction,no roots no *jouissance*
no reason to keep on going,bathed in poison rain
fungicide germicide suicide,forcefed junk syrup

denied their own Honey,like prisoners,refugees
immigrant workers who have become the World
chained to its own nonExistence. they Refuse

Chaos, I was called. *Chaos* meaning "chasm,gulf,
abyss, Hole" as the Greeks knew it my bloody self
the Moons menstrual bandage & what monsters
they think I am *....disorder in the atmosphere,in
the turbulent sea,in the fluctuations of wildlife
populations,in the oscillations of the heart & the
brain* "Chaos theory implies that huge changes
can be made using a minimal amount of effort" as
noted,& my eye shifts from Now to Then

and the brilliant light passes over

> I am the all-seeing Eye
> Whose appearance strikes terror,
> Lady of Slaughter, Mighty One of Frightfulness
> Who takes the form of blazing light
> I...most ancient female of the world

Egyptian Coffin Texts,from Spell 316

and the brilliant light passes over

the first wings were not paleAngels,flutter'd hands
at mute corners of Time,good women,the firstAngels
were FemaleDragons who erupted,spoke of Fire
parthenogenic Lizard,shark,snail &waterflea all
extend a Paradise,& take it back   All offer a
bargain,& change Her mind,*a rational leap into
fractal scream*

Flammantia moenia mundi sd Lucretius "the flaming
world walls" "....far-flung fortifications of Being
against Non-being" Robinson Jeffers,20th c. poet,
from "the unformed volcanic earth,a female thing"

and the brilliant light passes over

in Africa we are eating primates,gorillas,chimpanzees
logging roads open to men w/light,cheap weapons
semiautomatic slaughter kill the jungle there is a
market for "monkey meat" as one would eat ones
child,mother laughing without shame bullet tears
,or machinegun them to death for Nothing,because
that is life,a river thick with hippos,pigs or human
bodies stink all the same,in Africa as elsewhere,it
is time to eat ourselves,the hour of *ouroboros*
eating his delicious lunch,fat bulldozers order our
bones like gods, the time of mining whales for
dogfood,the seas all stink w/death,& will soon be
deserts as Men have dreamed in the great religion
of machines&War.breed children for Armies or for
food,or let them die to clear our continents,scrape
Africa etc flat&bare as a newborn planet,build
Industries of disaster that need disaster,disease
that feeds disease,manufacture Death to profit huge
tautologies of Money,eating pain &shitting pain
yr sole occupation,swallowing &shitting Death
your only food. ancient forests cut,upturnd soil,my
laboratory,library of bacteria virus medicine&raw
dream,what i once gave to hallucinate the simple
human,inchoate moods breed,replicate a rage like
butchering wild horses,men drive Kinshasa Hwy
across Africa ocean to ocean,trucks night&day ease
the long monotonous haul to nowhere fucking women
along the way,spread everywhere to the globe this
humusDeath my gift   my death,this humusGift
after a million years,you should have known

*Nature can be bored,*sd Rimbaud *After all, Nature
can be bored.*

"Donning the philosophical cloak,& making her way
thru the city,she explained publicly the writing of Plato
or Aristotle,or any other philosopher to all who wished
to hear…the magistrates were wont to consult her first
in their administrations of the affairs of the city,"
wrote my student,Hesychius the Jew

Thoth,god of writing w/head of baboon,mocked by
crowds of Christians who worshipp'd inanimate
Nescience,led by Theophilus,Bishop of Alexandria,
"God'sLove" *the nothing naughts he sd the nothing
naughts the darkening of the world forgetfulness
of Being* the god Serapis,statues shattered to bits
by a soldiers ax,orders of the same Theophilus
25 years before my murder before that,Temple of
Ephesus 550 bce,burnt&rebuilt destroyd&rebuilt,
Lady of Ephesus ancient Cretan,Artemis/Diana,her
priestesses call'd Melissai,the sacred Bees
until St Paul of Tarsus came to pray,cast out my
Demons,split my altar (Acts of John,2nd c.)rape my
heart,then 401ad a mob led by St John Chrysostom
finished it,erase the ruins

you are grabbed while removing sacks of groceries
from the car trunk you are an educated woman who
works harder but earns less you are not wearing a
dress they rip off trousers &blouse a long robe of
elegant cool limbs &w/religious hands they are in
shape of dirty spoons,violently opened oysters,the
consciousness ofHypatia is eaten breasts thighs belly
face,they scoop visions from yr eyes & especially(so
piously)drooling drooling they scrape out yr cunt
they enter the sea soft womb tunnels they grab
fistfuls of genetic future,& "When all is done: the
aphrodisia of the oysters' raw meat," eat you alive
current assassinations,intellectuals writers artists
the wonders of the world must not be wonder'd,my
Image,"idols" smashed by *Iconoclastes* who work
for God,Descartes, men of power&DeadEye(Dick)
Himself w/a DeadEye,hypnosis of human capacity
to obey a Lie,to render a world Dead w/stare of
aVoyeurist eye,as he masturbates his numbers the
glare of holy men,police,interrogators searchbeam
into the soft dark where we hide,always afraid,his
one power the stolen Medusa passion of earth's
ocular judgment,of My Eye

and the brilliant light passes over

and the brilliant light passes over

i am making copies of knowledge

*The whole world is knit & bound within itself: for
the world is a living creature everywhere both male
& female & the parts of it do couple together...
by reason of their mutual love.* – Giambattista
Della Porta, Magiae Naturalis, 1558

an erotic silence,as thought wanted,but my voice
gagged my legs open,the gift of Everything in
return for bitterness,even the celibate &the dead
require for his HeroicStory haw haw haw haw
"Woman is never anything more than the scene of
more or less rival exchange between 2 men,even
when they are competing for the possession of
mother earth." exhibit these wounds to the world
surely they will see the damage done. No,only a
mans wounds are sacred as the world is made of
Women,females are female,males are halfgirl
halfboy,thus men are jealous real women bleed
Alone

at the end,from caverns of fiends,dungeons w/
chains impeccable &cold as Thought,jewels
of dead animals i wear on my shoulders,the last
oryx the last gryphon the last river all i remember
they split me nakedly open pour'd out rain&
metal &blood,whole galaxies of spinning letters
nerves pulpfictions Zerofuturetheory unwritten
poem of the earths mind burned as witch witch
witch   strange&prophetic events,data of her
eyes,tongue,stature as she might walk now into
the public zone & speaking of it she is truly
dangerous to the holy man she is truly the
enemy ofMan   owlEyed,catcrouch'd,fragile
you are up for seizure,you have been SoldOff
the entire female Landscape is plotted w/the
NationalForest, old growth the wetlands the
immunity of frogs,gargoyles & vultures &

lemurs you belong to them yr lust & wit, the
radio spectrum of mass elucidation,silenc'd
birdthroat,scarab foot,scabrous&sleek limb,
the female voice   2000 nasty years dreaming
of it Apocalypse of Everything can happen
she sd,life being Real can Die
                          suck in the worlds
last breath,
          his enterprise to create My Death as
aReligion,erase this Brain a blank testament of
pages on which Extinction writes,the End

*& the Feminine voice reaching to the bottom of
volcanoes & grottoes of the arctic seas*

do not leave the copy place where we may reproduce
our selves as clarity in calm

Phase Transition:
*discontinuous jump in a system's behavior as a
parameter crosses critical thresholds*
 (e.g. ice $\diamond$ liquid $\diamond$ gas)
*Once a critical threshold is passed, the fire spreads
outward, the disease becomes an epidemic, the
material magnetic.*

Mandelbrot set

$$Z \Leftrightarrow Z^2 + C$$

Z iteration Z squared plus C
iteration: output of one equation becomes input of another

some old men masturbate into books their testimony
of venom,w/no Love,the fracturing spasms,power
tautologies   break theMind
& then the great reversal,the breathing of stars
                          women,the young,animals
will refuse. Earth will refuse the Use of her

body.   Some old mans brain becomes a big pot
of dust remove the pot it is entropy   remove that
it is Me
            CHORA or "receptacle" cf Plato's
cosmology [Timaeus] where it is "the mediating
instance in which the copies of the eternal model
receive their shape."
            *"this rhythmic space without thesis or
position,this process where SIGNIFICANCE comes
to be...."*

these are not Ideal forms but Nature,nor manmade
but Real "the broken, wrinkled & uneven shapes"
not Euclids thought,or pure God   solely mouth
tongue clitoris cunt brain ear eye(theFemale1100
genes,theMale50,the Egg *evolution*,the Sperm
residual)& then they burn us among our libraries
,runes & spells & rituals museums of codes
100,000 years of ice at the top of the world
dripping weeping tears into thoughts last pool
now at copy machine,somewhat like a womb
of parthenogenesis   copies & memory
DREAM ON/OFF
(X creates Y then takes it back)

Mandelbrot Set
          complexity generated by a simple act
          11010100001
                 on off on off black white up down
          simple reversals of time/space man/woman
          plus fluid complexities pain biology function
          the earth who dreams evolves to be self-
          desired in our Eyes
QuantumEpiphany bluegreen geometry color
          sound the quantum jump is my Mind
          all dials checked that signify
and push the button
and then there is the light and then there is the copy
the perfection of recollected lines pages texts the
code of absolute
                    transmission

and all the luminous sequences of,instruction of
clone machine which appear [new]genetic code

COPY

"....the COPYING MACHINE is a CLONING MECHANISM,
rather like the reproductive organs of the female....there is a
sensation that bellies are coming out of bellies"
  --Peter Greenaway, filmmaker, Belly of an Architect,
    interview 1991, in Arthur & Marilouise Kroker, eds.,
    The Last Sex: Feminism & Outlaw Bodies, NY: St.
    Martin's Press, 1993, p. 239

Sources:

Socrates Scholasticus: Margaret Alic, Hypatia's Heritage:
    A History of Women in Science from Antiquity to the
    Late 19th Century, London: Women's Press Ltd., 1986,
    pp. 45-6

The Parabolans, Cyrils Guard: Maria Dzielska, Hypatia
    of Alexandria (trans. F. Lyra), Cambridge & London:
    Harvard University Press, 1995, pp. 92-3

[i] was alive & living in Athens, Alic, p. 46

"the [last] pagan woman", John of Nikiu & Damascius, in
    Dzielska, p. 92

"and her body shamefully treated....", Hesychius in Suda,
    10th c. encyclopedia, s. v. Hypatia 4, quoted in Dzielska,
    p. 93

"Synesius saved himself by professing to be a Christian",
    Elizabeth Gould Davis, The First Sex, Maryland:
    Penguin Books, 1972, p. 240

"lack of witnesses", Alic, p. 46

Cyril thus "destroyed the last remnant of idolatry in the
    city", John of Nikiu, in Dzielska, p. 94

Bertrand Russell, History of Western Philosophy, London/
    NY: Simon & Schuster, 1941, p. 368

menstrual bandage anecdote: Dzielska, p. 50-3

Anna Spencer, Woman's Share in Social Culture, 1913

Wilhelm Reich, The Mass Psychology of Fascism, 1933;
    NY: Farrar, Straus & Giroux, 1971, p.105

Friedrich Nietzsche, The Anti-Christ, Section 22, 1888;
    UK: Creation Books, 2002, p. 37

"first order models of rivers....", Benoit B. Mandelbrot,
    The Fractal Geometry of Nature, NY: W. H. Freeman
    & Co., 1977, p. 68

"scientists look for things that obey laws....", Arthur M.
    Young, The Geometry of Meaning, Anodos
    Foundation, 1976

Media in the Czech Republic, January 1997, Jan Culik
http://www.arts.gla.ac.uk/Slavonic/Staff/CzechMedia3.html

Pharos, the lighthouse in Alexandria's harbor, one of
the "Seven Wonders of the World," built 290 bce,
destroyed by earthquake in 14th c.

"where every noble morality develops....", Friedrich
    Nietzsche, The Genealogy of Morals, Section X,
    1887. Slightly different translation in The Birth of
    Tragedy & The Genealogy of Morals, (trans. Francis
    Golffing}, Garden City, NY: Doubleday Anchor
    Books, 1956, pp. 170-171

"since, now, the core of the energy release....", Wilhelm
    Reich, The Murder of Christ, NY: Farrar, Straus &
    Giroux, 1953, pp 169-170

"most people don't find sex that pure....", Norman Mailer,
    Cannibals & Christians, NY: The Dial Press, 1966,
    pp. 197-198

"better off dirty, damned, even slavish!....", Norman Mailer,
    The Armies of the Night, NY: New American Library,

1965, p. 36

"You see, I think sex has always been dangerous....",
   Norman Mailer quoted, Anderson Valley Advertiser,
   Fort Bragg, CA, circa Oct 10-20, 1997

"The ONE God...." and "I cannot endure the way....",
   Friedrich Nietzsche, The Anti-Christ, Sections 40 & 44,
   UK: Creation Books, 2002, p. 62, 67

Mary Zeiss Starge, "A Dance for Chastity", USA Today,
   March 19, 2007, p. 15A, makes a Feminist argument
   vis-à-vis the patriarchal "Purity Balls." The Christian
   "Handmaiden" phenomenon appeared in the 1990s
   across America.

"the dominion which was liberty to her....", Norman Mailer,
   "The Time of Her Time" in Advertisements for Myself,
   NY: Putnam, 1959, p. 440ff

"Our treasure lies in the beehives....", Friedrich Nietzsche,
   The Genealogy of Morals, Preface I, (trans. Francis
   Golffing), NY: Doubleday Anchor Books, 1956, p. 149

See James Gleick, CHAOS: Making a New Science, NY:
   Penguin, 1987, p. 3

"disorder in the atmosphere,in...." Nigel Lesmoir-Gordon,
   Will Rood, Ralph Edney, Introducing Fractal Geometry,
   UK: Icon Books/ USA:Totem Books, 2006, p. 63

Spell 316, Egyptian Coffin Texts, R. T. Rundle Clark, Myth
   & Symbol in Ancient Egypt, London: Thames & Hudson,
   1959, pp. 221-224

Robinson Jeffers, The Selected Poems of Robinson Jeffers,
   California: Stanford University Press, 2001, p 690

"Nature can be bored....", Arthur Rimbaud, A Season in
   Hell, (trans. Louise Varese), NY: New Directions, 1961,
   p. 73

"Donning the philosophical cloak....", Hesychius the Jew,
   in Alic, p 45. quoted from Joseph McCabe, "Hypatia"
   in CRITIC 43, 1903, pp. 267-272

"the nothing naughts....darkening of the world....", Martin
   Heidegger, somewhere

"The whole world is knit & bound....", Giambattista Della
   Porta, Magiae Naturalis, 1558, in Carolyn Merchant,
   The Death of Nature, San Francisco: Harper & Row,

1980 (English translation), p. 104

"Woman is never anything more....", Luce Irigaray, in
    New French Feminisms, Elaine Marks & Isabelle de
    Courtivron, eds, NY: Schocken Books, 1981, p. 105
    (from Irigaray's This Sex Which Is Not One, Paris:
    Minuit, 1977; English trans. Claudia Reeder)

"& the Feminine voice reaching....", Arthur Rimbaud,
    "barbare," in Illuminations, (trans. Louise Varese),
    NY: New Directions, 1957, p. 103

Phase Transition: "discontinous jump...." "Once a critical
    threshold....", Lesmoir-Gordon, Rood & Edney, ibid.,
    p. 98, 103

"the mediating instance in which...." Jacqueline Rose,
    Sexuality in the Field of Vision, London/NY: Verso,
    1986, 2005, p. 153-154

"...this rhythmic space....", Julia Kristeva, in Jacqueline
    Rose, ibid, p. 154

"the broken, wrinkled & uneven shapes....", Benoit
    Mandelbrot, quoted in Introducing Fractal Geometry pg. 7

the blue rental

the missing girls

a building constructed by white sand,the deserts warehouse
Men go in &out,lugwrenches hammers a cement floor where
oil &water stain their boots as if blood &they are surgeons
of machinery. Noise muted,a radio of wind,everything is too
hot, sweat beads&mixes with black dust. a location far from
highways,there is a rusted sign somewhere& dirt road.Who
comes &goes has no name,a static business without any
advertisement on a 360 degree horizon
Men who work appear& disappear from the air,dressed in
blue overalls,tshirts, organic or mineral skin
what do they perform: aBeast chained to a rock like a dog
guarding a poison that drips from the sun
there are other buildings
Wheel depot, wall yard, home factory etc. Visceral metal
disconnected tubes pipes dismantled bathroom fixtures old
refrigerators frontdoors recharged batteries of empty rooms
somehow these bldgs are connected to the missing girls.
dont ask why
storm rain lightning mirage all very far away. Phenomena

bleached by distance.Weather occurs in a mind, not here,day
&night a lightbulb burns in a cage in a skull of a job manager
without shadow.This decides storm lightning heat mirage
what is done here: Coagulum of space/time
                                        the monster licks this
jewel slowly until the animal is so sick it can eat its own
death. & be full

Specifications: living things
thorax antennae wing what moves on their own,powered
by will ofMachine or that they move in dark heat,on foot
dawn has not happened,Engines of earth as black hum
abdomen lung bone begin to sweat before any Sun,as
engines believe movement upon earth is Alive
Specifications: long dark hair,small, thin, medium skin
ages 10-25
as any animal on its way to work or school,day or night
crosses the path of,random selection or destiny,what is
meant by,a science or a game

the Method
All is Object .of a cruel desert,a cruel god, predators eye
or job boss, any scent of flesh or automata(seeking like a
child to live beyond this)their residue scattered shoes socks
tshirts backpacks among rib femur skull in sparse lots or
retrieved into bldgs industry forensic charity used parts
on categories of shelves (dissected information)
                                        Alma,age 13,Irma 12,
anonima 8   mothers give names in love,these objects
return value as product,crime list,sensations of news,the
scent of a desert thicker than blood

bldg ofEvidence white powdery dust like a floor,strewn
w/specific things,rose blouse,earring rosary hair ribbons
name tag,new factory uniform,one dies clutching weeds,
or sand thick under fingernails one strangled w/own
shoelace vaginal &anal rape Esmeralda 13, Marina 11
white tennis shoes white panties carefully placed beside
or among grass & spikey weeds,mall bag w/parts of
trachea &a white bra,spinal column nearby,pelvis &parts

of a foot not far off black tennis shoe w/some bones of
the foot intact Cinthia 10, Ana Maria 11, Maribel 18
anonima 13, raped beaten tied to stake in playground
Guillermina 15, raped & burned alive,vaginal & anal
Susana Flores Flores 13, undergoes 4 heart attacks
during torture rape stab,strangle,gunshot to brain or
a hard yellow dirt the mystery of breasts,right breast
severed left nipple chewed off Adriana 15 anonima 13
anonima anomina 14,16,17 partly naked blouse & bra
pulled up over head exposing what remains of, ritual
mutilation
Parts&Appliances:this bldg composed of space,concrete
&absent walls & component parts strewn on assembly
tables flowers made from (her) genitals,mammaries,
eyes as some god spills jism which becomes a desert
Bat,it flies to the whore of Love bites it off,"that piece
of flesh" inside her vulva,which becomes Flowers .the
origin of flowers

aTempled bldg,as only men enter & leave. aloof from all
this their shoes black,polished & final Laws,codes,
documents of bullets are made here,the invention of God
& mechanicalReason the Worlds anatomy lesson begins
w/precision cuts as steps rise & fall into towers &
basements,silent ascent &descent into chambers &deep
hells,some wear robes,suits of authority,police,soldiers
priests,dealers in business,no eyes but shadows & in them
things disappear. what is meant by,aPower nothing
stops. Tire tracks left in night,or wrists bound by many
signatures,line after line in books which record &erase
their meaning,aLine of enormous pressure w/agony it
extends to horizons,crack open even dreams which are
unbearable Unknown things,to be silenced
                         a black car pulls
up,cowboy dressed in black,boots trousers shirt hat,a rifle
absolute w/history,gets out & performs its ceremony
they work for LaSantisimaMuerte most holy death
they say but there are no women here
                    boys enter a bldg no one knows,aVoice
gathers them up,the repeatedName chosen by something
like them but bigger,more angry a church,garage,an

armory where metallic things reproduce in cold light ,&
theEnemy,flesh,is molten & hammered & nailed as it
must be,toServe a progeny ofThis. the boys go in Alive
&come out changed,a drone of continuous wind becomes
theirMind, & wear as insignia,necklaces of little
flesh beads,girls nipples

Speculations: as (mirage)dwellings of cardboard,packing
crates plastic tarp barrels old tires,Factory trash piled &
angled among rocks&brush as if inhabited,animals or insect
colonies live there no running water windows doors,one
room they hang blankets to make walls,8 rooms many
animals or bugs hovelled together,to be human to eat
sleep mate beyond this .or school,or a job,a movie,dance
or romance as seen,*las revistas* a screw thru a bottlecap
makes a bolt,aFemale 12-16 makes a family worker,the
extension cords,crazy wires strung everywhere live wires
among shacks along ground,over dirt roads a lightbulb,an
iron, radio,tv some current runs like nerve spasm or fire
thru a common body,or electrocution .theExperiment of
rodents of heat& saguaro,a skeleton of fire at night to be
human,who lives here exists,by dream tumbleweed in
manufactured wind,each rises to become,4am or midnight
walks alone,a bus or desert terrain,arrives 7am 2am, 24/7
factories of towering gates,security booths, parking lots,
green lawns &vegetation,as if water ran in the river,or air
was not stench, & here they may aspire to be,toilets &
showers,cafeteria food,hot&cold faucets,discipline&wages,
the anonymous receive a nametag,w/a human name

      mingled,body parts,units ofAssembly telephones
cellphones ears&lips,plasm circuits nerve fibers,remotes
calculators tvs,her eyes a common screen,mute tongue
off/on Embotella dora de laFrontera Motores Electricos
Continental Mgft Co/Continental Sprayers,bodies fertile
w/ambition(need or fantasy)work as repetitive hearts sex
organs of technology as especially young &deft,esp
desperate,asHuman her labor creates a destiny,reflex of
muscle against its poverty,quick fingers of windowshine
& bug spray,a quick mind bldg industry Maytag Kmart
Sears ovens microwaves beds&sofas she inhabits casas

lindas,vidas hermosas none inhabit drag a people thru
naïve blood&dust,a mirage to live in Johnson&Johnson
DuPont Amway Kenwood Alco Honeywell A.O. Smith
real flowers,perhaps,a plastic vase,advertise a girls brain
waterheater,glass lined a girls skin
          where bodies found,broken machine parts
garbagedump,basura city its wind does not distinguish
dead things,junk,animal or human   face down,head
buried dirt road edge of RioGrande strangled,left in
plastic bag,AirportDeliveryHwy,JuarezPorvenirHwy(the
Future)in drainage pipe CasasGrandesHwy kilometro
19 PanAmHwy a sewage ditch,thermal electric plant
bottling plant,#11&#12 towers FedElectricCommission
railroad tracks partly buried inPEMEX sportsfield,or
empty lot behind FLUOREX(outdoor &grow lights)
behind FedElectricStation&Fluorex,body in streambed
approx 17.4 yards from tracks(victims 32% young
workers,also students waitresses storeclerks putas)the
FutureCity STRACTED LEAR FASCO HIPERMART
ELANEX ELECTROMEX AUTOVIDRIOS zone of
murder,abduction or dumpsite is anywhere boys,men
assume theFutureHwy,all theirs norteno,el automovil,as
Invincible(female workers,GM Ford TDK RCA Sony
Toshiba)all thisPower,her handprints all over,windows
that do not scream,windshield that sees nothing,car that
transports death w/happy music playing
                              whatever,bodies
naked,halfdressed,dead 1 day 2 weeks a year quickly
disassembled by heat,summer 110 degrees,or winter mice
coyotes,dogs chew flesh&bone,field rats esp nasal &ear
cartilege,24 hours,faces gone Rosalina,20,kept alive
10 days,lowered w/belt into ravine or 21.4 yards from
train overpass in a baseball field in a stream,on top of
bushes (she had one leg shorter than the other,15-17
severely beaten,massive bruise,50 puncture wounds)
or naked,15-17,found on top of a used tire near Cerro
Bola

The Necessity,first
     boxes of seed soil nutrients time sun beyond this)a bldg
about food a bldg about money. Nothing goes in or out

w/outMoney. (Marx: "No admittance except on business")
this is business
their body but a statue,an earthen machine formed by God,
by intention,for purposes of Use a bldg of philosophers
thinkingBusiness humanFlesh is the single largest biomass
on earth,it once wasTermites such is Life
Descartes nailed his wifes pet dogs paws to a table,tortured
it experimented dissected it alive *in search of a soul in*
animals which he didnt find,they only exhibit pain &as
Machines do not feel pain,nor creatures made of theRules
ofMechanics(which are ofNature ruled by God) .while
theFemale breeds flesh as insects,prolific &unruled,so to
engender contempt for plurality,thus Usable as disposable,
she makes them a breeder of bugs,meat houses,surgent
plagues of redundance *the largest single biomass on*
Earth,now human,it once was bugs a thinking man's
problem,to beSolved powerfully,w/profit& Thought

    as a vacant lot,weeds & noise,2 busy streets on either
side,continuousTraffic,a bldg ofOwners,Associacion de las
Maquiladoras,US export assembly plants,8 rotten things
laid out affront theBusiness that employed them,as if before
them a ritual offering,*victimas utiles* dump the bodies here
no mystery the Female body after death,or before breasts
severed,gaping vaginas even virgins after rape,virginalfaces
swollen &agape,or black masks desiccated,fists full of desert
where they grasp for something roots,tears,another alive
orReal nothing is there   *no mystery here*
These are my books,sd Descartes pointing to his room of
dissected animals   including the family dog nailed down
alive & tortured in search of a soul(never found)as animals
dont feel pain thought Rene the terrible sounds are of an
intellectual music only the Mind hears
this is business

& then she enters the bldg of ghosts Lote Bravo Lomas de
Poleo ServiciosPlasticos yEnsambles,the workplace the
deathplace,remembered all she assembles of sad little
pieces,novela de su vida Lilia,17,ValentinesDay,leaves a
downtown factory,her hands join watermassage parts,also
student,loves poetry,studies journalism also mother of 2,

nursing infant. Kept alive 5days while they feast on her
terror &milk,her pleas &tears a kind of milk,salt of cunt&
fleshbread *evidence of many*,more semen in her than all
others   beaten raped strangled,set on fire repeat breasts
butchered w/hot milk spurting out in particular her ghost
contemplates baby son far away,thru plastic orGlass,cries
&the rapists laugh,body of vacant lot over &over *reporte
sin novedad* nothing to report
or the one w/50 puncture wounds,no name,15-17,5'5"
Oct 3 1997, 27.4 precise yards from train overpass in a
stream in a baseball field on top of bushes,still has one leg
shorter than the other,anonima,it never changes   those
displayed w/arms chopped,8 carnal crosses,uniforms
close by   or girl,13,w/4 heart attacks enduring torture
she is still having them
one victims clothes tossed over mothers back fence,Cop
collecting evidence tells mother *la chavala andaba da
cabrona* that means yr girl enjoyed her sexDeath,his pene
grande,thus he pays himself la mordida,su cuota   police
handcuff marks on many corpse wrists .dramas
sell,what they love,to watch on tv & the pathos thereof
endless romance betrayal grief
& the ghosts understand,they were born to weep

*certain gods decide what is valuable what isnt. Human
pain,it is like killingEarth,raping Life eating theHeart of
Things,a big thrill   they are expendable,10,100,1000,1
million die so what? there are always more we know
where they come from,sd theMachine .& we know what
is happening to them & we understand.The awfulness is
eternal but necessary sd the god &all my begotten things
designed as sacrificial matter the idea is fulfilled when
each is opened up & emptied of whatever her name was
did she ponder did she dream no only of this moment
she is made for*
     a bldg of laundromats how clean&shining,at last
it must be heaven they are washing all the bloody clothes
because they cant stand aromas ofBlood putrido in a 10year
old murdered girls clothes,policeGuard uses perfumed fabric
softener to make the stink go away, it disappears like all
flesh,all evidence in the shining machines

barbara mor

        of theWest,wild horses(Wyoming Nevada Arizona)a
factory town built to slaughter horses for dogfood,the wild
beasts penned in cages,no shade,Sun sweating ,crazy in their .
eyes.Horseblood bubbled up thru wooden sidewalks,they all
smelt it workers &horses,the stench pervasive. Dogfood in
Japan, European steak, Dutch company, American profit
factory farming does destroy the sacred aura but hey
thats how the Market evolves,sd the butcher
this is business

raped.then they tied them &stuffed cotton in their mouths.
then they lit the cotton & burned them to death
in Darfur this is business   & the Hadji girl,14,Abeer,
held down,4 US soldiers go crazy on her,then shoot her in
head, bash her face w/cement block (shoot mother father 6
year old sister in next room)set the girl on fire,stomach to
feet,destroy semen evidence,her hair on fire &the family
pillow used   war is a business
sold over border intoChina,workers orSex slaves,some girls
bound in leather harness&5 times daily immersed in Leech
ponds   the leeches suck their blood,then at end of day are
harvested for market,big fat leeches get top prices.Parents
choose the strongest daughter,prettiest daughter,the most
loved or difficult daughter her sale into sexWork orLeech
trade can feed rest of family for a year
        this is a business
a mother distraught over problems,personal&money,walks
into a lake holding 4 year old daughter,8 year old son by
the hand.The boy swims away &lives,mother w/girl in her
arms drowns   SummitLake, Akron Ohio she couldnt take
it anymore it is all a business

 in the case of severed heads which we can see moving &
biting the earth shortly after having been cut off,altho they
are no longer animate, ... sd Rene
orEmily Allison Miranda,other names   Manufactured in
a bldg that is the heat metals generate rubbing together
in wet dreams,objects who aspire toFame via Murder
made for aCulture &then they are gone   Brooke Ashley
Olivia,interchangeable as disposable,the one decayed

140

body folded in an appliance packing crate the other girl
stuffed in a kitchenFreezer,many weeks,then buried under
backyard barbecue,under a cement slab approx 10' x 10'
behind the house one is buried,space for a charcoal brazier
or maybe pingpong table in the summer.another is in the
freezer wrapped in plastic against the garage wall cool
in there most of the time

the excess of female bodies
manufactured for aMedia,nightly news tormented body
parts w/identities still missing or the search in swamps or
urban galleries alleys artloft imagination the surfeit of
subjects to be objects like chromosomes embedded await
a person to be thought about

or someone stops at a café along the road,looks for aGirl
hearing a girl is missing or maybe she is bound up in his car
trunk already dead or waiting to be dead.Ubiquitous heat
slows down everything even crime,murder slows to utter
dream An hallucination good people speed on thru while it
hovers in stopped Air&is seen by eyes already dead only
aVision only dead eyes see while good people speed thru
nothing seen as in a cemetery or autopsy lab or museum
no mystery here

what is lost when a work is massively(re)produced,that is
Art,or animal what is lost an *aura.* something on theLine
of assembly,manufactured energy, *laFlor sin magia* opens
petals of cheap flesh,Cash fucksTrash,business isBorn
orLife in age of material dissolution

*the bodies showed signs of torture,*as
aSaint plucks feathers,one by one, from aLiving bird to
demonstrate how God does not interfere when a Holy man
torments Nature,one reason or another,torture of Nature a
Game or religion among some,a Science,*these are my proofs*
*sd Descartes,*dead dog exhibit of myBrain
a bldg of philosophers,merchants discuss the nature ofMan,
rhetoric of Morality,the price of thought,price of pain,the
amount of unknown in the mind in theUniverse ofTime,the
cost of shoes&underwear in Juarez something dead inside
as the Picton BC pig farmer,rapist & murderer of dozens
of them(whores) chopped them up&mixed ground human
parts w/slaughtered pigs(very similar taste)so the missing

girls are in yr hotdogs lunchmeat&liverwurst,even so,all
the missing dark matter is still not
accounted for

*sometimes,they sd, when you cross a shipment of drugs to
the US,* crack the border,vate,*adrenaline is so high you
want to celebrate by killing women*
hot & heavy on the desert is redundant but these are cold
hearted bastards these are pricks of ice
*this is how he says,I only do it to bitches who deserve it
like God he decides who deserves it.this is how God was
manufactured in the black sweating place between the
scrotum & the brain the crease of grease & hair he says
the difference between God & nothing*
                    is theFear running up her spine freezing in her
eyes the shivering of small things at mercy of power they
enjoy briefly but never long it must repeat again &again
punctured &gulped down on the desert a mouse into
a snake open a cold beer after,yr
tongue explodes

Speculation,specification:
because the town smells like shit
                    a boy crouched in dirt which is aHome,littered
w/dead things,car noise,household refuse,chicken bones,
egg shells, *ratas* gophers(they can be eaten)carcasses of
dead dogs too common to be buried,children play among
them w/out differentiation. Human waste w/desert rain
washes down from elevations into a dirt valley,no trees
nothing multiplies but quikMoney &this human garbage,a
piss stream ofTrash   theIndustrial mirage,blurs w/
blown sand,oil fumes,refineries Alchemic burnoff,the
fetid sewers,air stinks of animal meat grinding inEternal
teeth,21st c.Machinery because the town,Life,smells
like cold shit,he wants revenge for the stink *wherever
people* they string electric cords together until they
reach theSun *theBeast drinks theSun* he squats in mother
dirt & his puppy is dead he holds it like a little girl a doll
indistinguishable from all else,skin junk dust wherever
people,because his river is a dead ditch,his eyes are not
of children *theMachine has touched the moon there*

is no stop only the desert is clean,& the smell of metal
that little girl inside him,that once trustful who must be
disabused,pierced& spat on,cut,crushed as she was in
him *pobre nino pobre hijo* he too was a pure child in
the beginning of theWorld the species w/Mind or Soul
Compulsed to experiment on those lesser,or none theBoy
alone in dirt w/women&dogs whose pain isUnreal yet the
screaming endless in his search forTruth,alone, wills
to be a monster in the image ofGod,i.e. the one who
forced him to be born from a human Organ *only the
desert is clean,the smell of metal. thoughtAlone*
        & some are so young 4 & 8 no sex
shows the hairless pubis the thin arms,bare chest&penis
of a child all this time only a mirror only one who shows
you a face you dont want to see,the inside girl little sad
puta lost puppy(curled up naked &whimpering) yr lost
heart yr poor little sad lost boy his little dead puppy
perrito cachorro cria & he is of course
the missing girl

Descartes only child Francine died,age5,scarlet fever it
was said he carried around w/him all times everywhere a
lifesize automatic replica of her body

Specs: (stains, residues,remains, after images,dust on the
lens)
if this isTime the haunted desert,dead girls wash up on
the sand daily,from all places,Intact or they are displayed
interchangeable items,a product ofDesign everything
we use& touch becomes,a value we forget *movements of
animals may be compared w/those of automatic puppets,
sd Aristotle* embodied in aGirl,the disconnected parts
limbs,clothes shoes bra of one discovered on another,&
someone is playing aJoke,because as if theKillers are
girls playing w/dolls or the dolls areDead girls playing
alone,aGame of murder beyond this, Emptiness
orSpace, scorpion &rattlesnake lizards dust crawl over
them,or inside a gravesite vase where theirFlowers are
plastic for nothing grows here,or survives theSun as
they cannot leave,it is aHome
all bones w/out flesh reveal theMachine *the reduction*

barbara mor

of the hearts movement to a mechanical operation no
mystery here except theGirls remain

   they stood in line for the job &managers w/cameras
snapped photos of them,theInterview process he sd, &
they disappeared,notAlive again a photo of something
dispersed into terrain,pieces which could be animal,or
human or some other planets vegetation.aCamera stops
a process takes nature away,fromDying fixes a crime of
Being as nothing has a soul everything is soul theDesert
is soul w/murdered girls strewn &desiccating

let us imagine(if we can)a female body stretched toAll
horizons,naked sand as aFlesh composed of all atrocities
done,Autopsy photos school &baby snapshots movies of
dreams,pornography torn fashion poses &Everything
sd in curses&Literature,delusions ofHeat &ornaments of
pain it shimmers as a gauze of,Eons pureImage,*objetos
puros* the pupil contracts& widens,asDeath,the brains
aperture her appearance in the killersEye as she vanishes
from theHuman,sinews strained toUnderstand or nude
skulls w/mouths wide open,screaming a power orHowl
as they become theWind *Sagrario Rosa Paloma*

theEyes pigment is dark purple,not black,notNight,as
some make things go dead in their eyes but theyContinue
to see   theExtended dead,*the flow pattern of spirits
streaming out of the pineal gland* we observe them
we see what others do not perhaps we are dead

   often air tastes like motor oil, or bread or speech
tastes like drilled oil.Or flesh tastes like gasoline or
   all things become fire or yr eyes iridesce in rain
clings to fatal intersections

we are not lost here,it is the rest ofLife fades a person,
a history,a mirage as terrible blood of theSun drips
   out& spreads,is disappeared into the surrounding
stain,as night

theImagination cannot escape the desert it is the final
place

144

the blue rental

****

Online Back Story:
Esther Chavez Cano & the Casa Amiga Crisis Center
(which she founded) compiled lists of female bodies as
they were found, "Murders of Women in Ciudad Juarez,
1993-2000," available at http://www.casa-amiga.org.
Updates from 2002 are also available on this site, which
has English translations. One of the components of the
Juarez horror is the collusion/incompetence of the whole
police & justice system, so information has been grossly
& often deliberately garbled. Several "reasons" for the
murders are offered, relating to the existence of Ciudad
Juarez as both a NAFTA site & a major drug crossing
site on the US border: the alignment of corrupt & inept
police, both local & federal, with the narcotraficantes;
the alliance of maquiladora businesses & both local &
federal politicians with both the crimes & their coverup;
revenge against women making wages & gaining some
independence from traditional male control; sons of
rich & powerful families, Los Juniors, who indulge in
thrill crime without fear of punishment; factory bus
drivers, Satanic cults, international organ trafficking; all
of the above. Altho news attention & human outrage,
Mexican & international, has brought greater scrutiny to
the crimes, many young women are still missing, most of
the murders remain unsolved, & the murders continue.
Solid online overview of the subject is found in Jessica
Livingston's Frontiers 2004 study, Murder in Juarez:
Gender, Sexual Violence, & the Global Assembly Line
[available on Google]; also Janice Duddy's What Is the
Connection Between NAFTA and the Murders of Maquila
Women? at Assoc. for Women's Rights in Development
site, http://www.awid.org/eng/Issues-and-Analysis/Library
plus that title

Material sources:
The Daughters of Juarez, Teresa Rodriguez, Diana Montane
& Lisa Pulitzer [NYC: Atria Books, 2007] "....when you cross
a shipment of drugs into the US" unidentified newspaper quote,
256 / Puro Border, editors Luis Humberto Crosthwaite, John
William Byrd, Bobby Byrd [El Paso, TX: Cinco Puntos Press,
2003] Sam Quinones, "The Dead Women of Juarez," 139-52, &
work of Esther Chavez Cano, 153-58 / Juarez: the Laboratory
of Our Future, Charles Bowden [NYC:Aperture Foundation,
1998]. On Descartes & dogs, 98 / Treatise of Man, Rene
Descartes, trans. Thomas Steele Hall [Amherst, NY: Prome-
theus Books, 2003] 2-4, (Aristotle quote, p 4, note 5), 51
(note 89), 81 (note 130) / A Discourse on the Method, Rene
Descartes, trans. Ian Maclean [Oxford, UK: Oxford U. Press,
2006] 45, 46 / Christina of Sweden, Margaret Goldsmith
[Garden City, NY: Doubleday, 1933] "These are my books,"
112 / Reference to Karl Marx, Capital, Vol. 1, trans. Ben
Fowkes [London:Penguin-NLB, 1976] 279-80 / Fragment
of quote from Roland Barthes, The Fashion System, "Let
us imagine (if we can) a woman covered with an endless
garment, itself woven of everything said in the fashion mag-
azines," in The Postmodern Scene, Arthur Kroker & David
Cook [Montreal: New World Perspectives CultureTexts
Series, 1986, 1987, 1991] 132.

the blue rental

oasis3

the small blue man a small man tends the door,he wears a
blue jacket,all is glassy silence bldgs &parkinglotEmpty,the
sun exists at some angle to the sky the small blue man is
almost not there,he is Tokwah who opens the door
                                        as many years,the
close world,vinous enclosed &moistured green film,earth
enwrapt in its sweat &thick creations,who is mouth,stink
&eating who is water(jaguar,Fire) in a jungle of entropic
things he thinks he is many dreams all sensate cells,all
skins explode,Omnivorous of desire elderly blue person,or
shrunk white man,all thats left, arthritic &hypnotic,at the
turnstyle inside the door(inside the plaza inside the
wonder)aGreeter,can barely stand or move yet humbly
mechanical for the job,the doors of automatic sliding
glass,of hisEyes,open beyond mortality *&theSilence*
everywhere that was aWorld flesh floor,liveMezzanines
of air,anaconda flowers rain eyes lickt day&night w/
paradise,bodies consuming the display of bodies
rapturous or w/out commentary,except orange purple

yellow noise explosions in anOracular skull he counts
fireants crocodiles bats millipedes piranhas,ecstatic
merchandise heThinks bright red blood eyes as a bird
flies up this parrot screeching words &becomes a clever
man *there was aTree,ocean in aTree,Tokwah hooks
out a great flood & everything drowns*,rivers pour out
his orificesPissing& preachingFever his monkey tricks
penetrate himself,a slippery muscle poison always
lustful always hungry &mens *milk*,intercourse w/
toads,a thorn in the squirmy anus extrudes secretion
abundantly,dipt w/petals on penis& theMind he makes
semen the invention of(adultery &murder)
                    *so that you remain dead,so
that you are dead,he madeDeath,thisBrain glows in the
dark,binocular &cruel,scares away return ofGhosts
until theWorld closes,now they come*
some say Tokwah is a little man   he thinks he is many
animals in this desert jungle of fish,frutas,money &
circularTime(you will become)a blue glow pervasive as
mythic 1stThought,or not   a shrivelled old man,ancient
One guide to some Futuro suburbano *Bienvenidos
al mercado de la Ultima Parada* he does not speak
                         he has a tool to zap
you to aVoid if you look crosseyed(& are not Mayan)
sometimes he wears dark glasses they are mirrors theEyes
are mirrors solely &there is no longer any need to smile
he is Tokwah Lord of Death
welcome,enter & become the world

                    ****

the world in fact is empty now,but this lucent space
retains all yr best features   laCiudad delDiosShopping
Mall,la galeria as plexigalaxy unspirals yr dizzy brain as
stars,planets,landscapes, 3story fullfurnished houses
*pinnacles domes iglesias kingly halls,Babylon walls&
gardens*(simulations),the illusion of having everything at
once in one place,&Affordable boutiques,Banks tacobars
juicebars,theaters ampitheaters moats balconiesArches
over balconies,bridges Pyramids,enchanted tattoos,jewels
hair salons bra&pantie emporiums egyptEngineers of

the blue rental

profiles& sacred echochambers inhabit these facades
foudroyant &fatal,yrDream as only life could be if
elaborately decorated
        atrium of light &*air like light*,a violet effusion
      of floral escalators & those now risen,transported by
        invisible wires or dispersed as from perfume
        atomizers the angelic realms,neoplastic realms
      spilling glassy rivulets&neonic fires *chalets of crystal&*
      wood that move along invisible rails&pulleys (poetic!)
        asSpirits recapitulate an old ambition to
      move from shop to shop aisle to aisle thing to thing
        unimpeded by humanity
ascendent fromAmnesial bowers(shadowy)
of sculpted ivy& stone flowers,the incorporeal
adrift in luxury *resembling nothing that is yrs*
no little monkeyturds or quetzal or pigeon flyovers,
squalls,words,sweaty brains,hands seeking money
    mortify pleasures of naturalHallucination,or
    criminal dogs howling in the mud streets
    a violent air eviscerates w/spires of faux metallic
      fingers the atrium w/light plunged down into the
pool,the food court the toilets &lounges&basement
    ventilators,odors of any lifeforms dispersed long ago
        into atmospheres of dryOblivion as
    yr bodies into *gaping graves* (airconditioned)
        as aMirror,the pool,Mayan azul(an
    allusion)*a strange city upsidedown in the dimWest,*
    its emptiness anEye not yet open to the public,or
      closed forever,as in bankruptcy ofMind,
    lo! 2 figures(*dead w/out tears)the melancholy waters*
    uphold them,bobbing,swimtubes &sodapopcans
    &*the collapse of apotheosis*,just like the old days
LosDos,elEdgar&elArthur their dark sunglasses
    are mirrors w/smoke rising from them,slowly
    coiling as if anEternal cigarette (who invented that?)

    ah! you dont need to exist to enjoy this

day,night the eternalClimate nothing that breathes,or
tarnishes aSilence something crawled here from Silurian
seas,started a business,a motel a scorpion church,altars

de la comida,sexo,Weekend relaxation & only the people
fuck it up,so they are gone no philosopher orShopper
looks minutely down or up in search of a *raison d'etre,*a
bargain,a chilidog(whateverIt was for) no,solamenteLos
Dos y sus companeros,Huginn&Muninn(black invisible
birds) laidback in wet azul,Art&Ed ,as pagan sadistic
recurrence circles the world,7Up orSplice in one hand w/
maybe those little pink umbrellas,or technicolor straws,&
sometimes *the waves glow red* &spin them around,*el vahido
del vacio,*it makes them dizzy(in a fun way) at poolside,
2 chaises longues(plastique!),2 terrycloth beachrobes(250
million years from an ocean),one lifeguard sign:
    Art might find some viewers objectionable(Ed2)
nothing makes them happier than poquitoMariachi
music in their heads(nobody hears it) &dos cuervos
fly over&over this uninhabitedSpace w/out even being
there
              ****

what a place!

erupted magmas,volcanoTemples&mountains,dinosaurs
rumble around a lake in *la caldera,*1 million years(bigger
than a futbol stadium)then laAgua dries up,grassy land,a
car lot,mastodon tiger camel minihorses roll down the
boulevards,new&shiny until this also dries up,Rust&
extinction,inside aSun that turns all juicy hearts toStone
    assorted cacti,lizards,rats y los espiritus retirados
live here now,Lifestyles de losMuertosGringos, una tren
de vida consumida
         the deserted world,very spacious,black
roads exude from the sacredMall complex into sacred
    *alrededores,*landscapes of rock,magnificent houses
of glass&rock,glamorous suburbs of melted sand
    w/active birdwings &agave blades embedded,a
primitive nature cultivated w/superbArt (thank you)
1000 vago driveways,stript &white,1000 backyard pools,black
    in the unobserved night,light fromSirius orVega orOrion
reflects in their stagnant waters& eyes of coyotes who
    watch theSpirits gather around the dark barbecue,the
lounge chairs &patio ramada,everything intact for

the blue rental

luxurious desert living
LosDos,here&there,appear (quantumly)lounged,empty in
turquoise dream,for they do not swim except in this
aqua,their disembodied brain,the blind one too thin to
float &the thin,blind one has nowhere to go it is enough
to recline&wonder at the completeVacancy of el world,the
unoccupied silence,abstract blue upon black&black of the
unironic sky,night aereated by neon(glances of eyes
in thought)or not (closing of heavy lids onEternity,a
brief nap) soArt&Ed on lawn chairs w/shotguns across
pellucid laps,ready to shoot anyThing that lives(gringos
behind every bush,allHorizons,a video hallucination)&/or
they populate the pool w/companions,blownupdolls(blond
o pelirrojo),pterodactilo &yellowDuckies &when
it comes to the Az/Mex Border,exactly what is a *Hot Spot?* a
CriminalHotSpot?? lawn chairs? lawn chairs???
we aint got no stinking lawn chairs theres no lawn!!!
as gentlemen savages,*i.e.*LosDos,*hunt their news by the
light they have invented*

theAfterlife,all thats left,dreamt of *theEternalWest* &
built in yr fear ofDeath(rightly so!)lost somewhere here
among Dos Cabezas ySuperstition,Catalina&Chukson,
themepark celebrity museum gatedCemetery whatever,a
sunkenMoon w/drunk gods sleeping offForever in hotels
&motels of paradise no one has to change the sheets,&
shopping mall of Toltec ruins w/ghosts going up&down
stone escalators   *amid the life,moving of itself,of that
which is dead* sd Hegel(how did he know?)
             a planet abandoned,cities
housesEmpty of superfluous flesh,yr evacuate rooms
factories hospitals,sad highways &lunar highrise,wept
as deserts upward& alone,theSpirits come,retire,the
dry air resembles them ,*all winds all years all days* all
Straight lines,roads progress intoHeaven,like aCrashsite
in *el cine teleologico*   theVehicle theMind the Place
the house,the car in its house next to the house,the
epistemeWho failed to exist as thisOtraVida would be
ruined by yr living body,skin floated,flaccid,florid,yr
loud dispersers of ancient blood flowing down stone
stairs &stone faces *to its quietude*

theSpirits enjoy the same things (*so many have
given their hearts!*) golfcourses,faux lakes &palmtrees
sacrificial altars,boudoirs,kitchens zoologicMenus
,spectacles ofAges of struggled matter into all that
doesntMatter,beast after beast walking intoFire,tusks
feathers pelts fins hands fingers tongues
devolve inFire,*conflagrations ofSky,*the pleasures of cloud
&light,induced images that become theHours,the
pleasures of opening doors,sinking into swirling hot
maelstroms,emergent from sulfuric oozes,lungfish swarms
of flies &cocoons as furry bodies from the maternal
ch(i)asm(u)s *the most tremendous failure of time* sd
WWhitman (how did he know?)

ixiptlas, those little makeshift things who represent a god
2 sticks tied together by spit a human hung on a horizon 2
bleeding sticks who cares,in the long run there have been
so many   *LosDos the last men do not care* what is
manufactured lasts longer than what lives
merely *so perfect you have to use drugs to endure it*

there are reasons for the tall locked gates & stonefaced
walls,theDying now only bones pile up against them as if
left from a tidal wave,or the postperson at xmas,pkgs from
some season,or the remains of a feast of dogs

****

on theMarket,these wondrous abodes creators of worlds
may dwell in,as if(suggestions of Earth dwindling down
to a house)astride toilets englowd w/stainglassshowerdoors,
or fuckt bestride the bestThighs of beds&Dominion,persons
may be artists or gods,or gaze thruOblivion,feel so much
better aboutThemselves& speak words that relate them to
bodies &stars of sumptuous orbits around a flat rim,that
desert appearing again &again,in some whiteEye aimd
too long at theSun you can watchRoads &sand &beasts
&Time dissolve into each others form,&billions squat in
their dust to die,as If(life dwindling down toEnd)

in the meantime you may enjoy *Delusions bigger,w/*

more rooms 13+ annexes!for each occasion!w/fewer
occupants!uncluttered vistas! imagine yrself royalty to
wanderAristocraticallyRooms for entertainment&special
uses MediaRoom,GameBoxRoom,PoleDancingRoom,
CasinoRoom,SushiEatingRoom,OrgyRoom(aHousewife
issue)Glutrooms of variant items&Idols *in order*,genre
to species,faces2spaces,feel&reveal,a clear border in&
out between tools& moods,moods &ambience,Taste is
paramount when it no longerExists,i.e. aDeSadeRoom
always on opposite sides of familyrecroom from the
Disney/SpielbergAlcove,WarRoom*west* &Chapel*east*
&so forth easier to keep clean,walk-inMurderRoom for
example is on a diagonal wing from the KitchenRoom
&FuckGym but each has its own discrete scrub crew
 (twice a week)(Guatemalan)(on alternating days)(maybe
the same people)w/pantrywings containing implants vital
to each obsession,& a funeral viewing room for family
wallowing if desired *Opposite* theBirthingRoom its all
here,the world   *6000 feet aboveMan*,breathtaking
our marvellous plastics,you who are made of plastic&
cannot live beyond vicarious flesh,lascivious positions
&feel of superiorVinyl,you may escape in our luxurious
foams,Lifestyles of theNoLongerHere every house a
vast foyer entrance w/winding staircase & yr limbos
goingUp& down,lowclass spirits yearning for highclass
sensation *towels bathrobes blankets in their deleuzian*
folds aNest w/4walls smeared w/VictorianHindu&Asian
pornographies,ceilings ofMirrors,interactive wetdreams
w/all Unreality as if there is any difference between a
dick&a dildo aThing or aThought spasmodic digitals
almost like silk skin 1million pixelcount bedscreens
where you can be theStar of something &the satin lacy
feel between yrthighs rubbing together that is the point

up there,w/feet in the waterfall&brambles,stags suckled
atDianas breast a huge blowup ofVanGoghs A Pair of
Boots w/lifesize CGI imposition of almost nudeParis
Hilton draped erotically over the upright(undone)shoe
her arms&hands embrace a soiled bootlace as if naked
masculine shoulders while her tongue licks atLeather
obscenely meanwhile that poquito chihuahua tugs so

playfully at the sprawling sad shoelace which if pulled
indefinitely will unravel what exists of her thongpanties
&from therePubic hair &whatever lies under that for
this is a selfreflective art always already *sous-rature*

bacchantes of the suburbs sob&the moon burns&bays
(French!)on the radio you can hear men screaming as
they are dragged off to prison cells,deathsquads,church
picnic stonings help me god i dont want to do it &
these are old taperecordings wedontknowwhathappens
next but veracity givesEdge to predominantly soothing
CDmusical performances&ersatz rainforest sounds *out
of castles built of bone comes mysterious music* & here
are videos of women jumping screamingUp&down or
crowds cheering or singing inChoirs or DVDs of small
animals being spikd crushd pulpd by black stiletto heels
&squeals of pain are hard to distinguish from squeals of
women winning newTVcars or a trip toHawaii or those
pervasive Rx orgasms   everyday is anApocalypse for
someone

        suspended here in a cacti& mirageVoid sparse
just as you like it neighbors &visitors are available,see
theScreenRoom storagecabinet &/orBluRay rack it is not
necessary to communicate w/other lifeforms at random,
on appointment or as daily unavoidable interface,*only
when you want it* this sensorium isYOURS,theDesign
is not to invoke,never provoke guilttrips of the past have
been met by yr personal AutoVirusGuard& immolated
this is a guarantee of use,see small $ print pg. 5649 of
UsersManual that means yr hand like God intends,signs
on,resigns all right of further MindChange UNLESS that
is a further program agreed to bySelf exists in motion,as
labeled either SURPRISE ME! or Shit, What....that
there are no on/off switches lets you know we areAll in
this together thru2theEnd – Others? part of the fascination
is the ongoing &/or recurring wonder,that &/or Question
(not of marvels)if anything left beyond you exists,is
there,at such a distance,it would, hardly matter – life
perchance on other planets galaxies or a town over the
horizon, irrelevant concerns for youll never reach them
or they you not in this place not w/this system others

are possible but then you never know

LosDos of course they are obsessed w/eating as many
exotic flavors textures blood suppurations as they will
consume before all colors& Fixtures &skins are gone,*as
always empty always hungry* compulsive filling up of
all the holes *the cunt the rectum the mouth the eyes the
nostrils the ears the bellybutton*   6 billion years of
Evolution,difficult for 2sticks who cant get enough all
the good things ofEarth in OurTime,devoured as
stuffd in a dark bag ofNothing matters
     the cosmic erotic it wants to go on forever we want it
to go on forever put it on aLoop recline& luxuriate in
theMobius of sunset midnite noon stars moon sunrise
over&over etc etc etc &yr glass of wine tea coffee beer
bourbon overflows w/out a bottom no discernibleEnd,in
search of aHappyEnding

****

*tezcatlipoca whose slaves we are
mocker, capricious creator,smoking mirror
lord of the here & now, muy cerebral& fickle*

you see,Mr Tezcatlipoca misspoke himself he did not sew
dogheads to dogbutts to make our first ancestors,rather,
Tata&Nene,the 1st couple,he cut off their heads to stitch
these to their human butts to make the first dogs,a big
metaphysical difference here? probably not   in either case
these perros made by Senor T were our first ancestors
not much difference
i think not
1st man & 1st woman survive the 4thSun,a great flood,but
only as 2dogs
Tez,he will not let anything have a happy ending

before the great flood (everyone has one)(or earthquake or
drought or famine or plague etc) theUtensilsRevolted   pots
knives ladles needles rocks rebelled against the people&
ate them up
theSun eclipsed,or the Moon, &the hammers &soupspoons

devoured them
&before that,1000 years all the weapons& personal items had
elbows,you were born from theKnees of gods(or a greatEgg)
or the toothbrush &the garagedoor opener of thefuture
devour you,just like a piece ofRope &a warclub drag you in
to get yr heartRemoved for the Big Owl
&night is locked up inside a plastic bowl,w/a blue lid, & lots
of stones &planets &useless things roll around inside
suchDarkness for a trillion years
Moyocoyatzin Titlacahuan Moquequeloa

we know you are not happy god is not working for you
rather the reverse of course we chichimecSons of theDog
we are here to make the unknown known a sad project for
then the story is done(we are done)
      El Ciego & El Oculto discourse:
        this sounds like a chiliasm
        a chili what?
sabemos inside all is,also, *deja vu deja la* Interior decor of
sus sesos maybe he is French or el dio delTedio
whatever   *speaking of food*
they fill up empty cargo container ships w/cardboard,los
americanos, & send them to China   &China uses the
cardboard to make streetsnacks,a little softener, spices &
chemical flavors yum yum but 65% cardboard
it all recycles
whereas on these empty streets Wacko&Sucko sell Pishtacos
(no more fish no more sea) that is,Pishtaco (rhymes w/
Dorado) is a little white man he has white skin& he kills
&cuts up los pobres,removes the face&the heart etc
to use their bodyfat for fuel   car gas airplane gas it works
or also some kind of antiseptic lotion,good for spider
bites   or mosquitos,everything bites
el fin delMundo es solamente un bocado poco

they have a hard time understanding elSol deNoche,a
BlackSun it is elementary,porque LosLosers,w/famous
nonambiguous brains they shake,shiver,shatter into many
pieces,sad plastoid chunks their littleLegos y suenos
elEstupido diddles his gold watch,Pensamientos delOro&
golden faucets *no agua no juicio*

everybodys a comedian

he stood before the god naked for 4 days,spread out in
*metaphysical guts&blood of the slippery place,*that is,our
sacred *karaoke,*a tlatoani moves hisTongue when the
god speaks,or a snake wants toSing,or sell some thing *theres*
a hiss or a hum when heEnters the brain   if you think god
is not aJoker you got the wrong desert gringos   &so when
consumers no longer have *sentido* to buy,supply meets
demand w/solution items: guns razorblades ropes suicide
pills,duel use pillows[*Sleep & Endless Sleep*]   for surely
you know thisPlace belongs to,pues, OurBoy
The Enemy on Both Sides (Schizo&Rhizo)
welcomingFlesh(&/or bones)from both sides of the border

you see,Tez,he will not let anything end well

All that will collapse   electric wires &babble,cuteStuff
(warzones superstorms suffocation by animal carcasses)
Tokwah shut out ghosts (who became businessmen) &
now we are Full & you are Emptied & now we are
everything & you are not,ourBusiness closed,transaction
complete deal concluded done   gone   *adios*
stunned in yr home or casa,it passes on a screen or offers
itself to perception like women or other goods,all the
places where people were standing moving ahead behind
lunchcounters carwheels guns clerks prettygirls soldiers
bankers tanks bulldozers(who sought not a place to live
but to feelAlive) globe as a village,village a shoppingmall
house is a room room a box,Box of assorted brain neurons
of spectators of history like dying persons it passes thru
aSkull as if already gone,Life from so far away does
it matter inside yr appointed *caja* you dont care,Spirits
do all this in ourCabezas,that you were embodied was not
a punishment but an achievement,Gracias! su cuerpo
in theFuture just blocks theViews
                                        a marvelousAfterlife
in yr human dream ofThings,behind every illusion a
blue screen &that hum,like distant insane machinery,what
they are scraping from yrSky is not tears but dust,dust
older than theSun,dust that was the bottom of some

barbara mor

originalSea (of dust)

& when he laughs,look out

you can still dip in the sea, i.e.
the dark sea of awareness except there is no water,Carlos
no water no water we have warehouses lots of beer&coke
etc you can desalinate yr tears or drink piss out of yr bare
hands too bad we ran out of paper cups(no trees) in the
desert we drink each other,lowly things eat higher intellect&
vice versa,mushrooms eat professors,PhDs eat toad shit
yr shit that glows in the dark
                 a chili ad?
far out in space,some other world reads this neon desert
like an advertisement
Sr Baudrillard,a smart guy,figured that out

what the next Sun will be who knows   LaAspiradora
enormousBeing,sleepless beyond sleep   a blue smoke rises
up,scent of copal allThings are painted w/this blue stare
before sacrifice,it comes from afar   what is time,Space
moving thru itself like a machine,drone of galactic
space like an approaching vacuum cleaner,theMysterious
Housekeeper tickling yr ass w/a broom   maybe it
snores,a hum like a peaceable kingdom

here we are in a deserted shopping mall in a suburb in a
world,a small blue man runs a vacuum cleaner in a room
before the final door
                 Mictlan tecutli,DeathLord whose domain is
The Place of No Exits
   all beyond behind this old blue man is emptiness
   if you really want to leave hell open the door for you, i.e.
   at the end there is no more just a shrunken little blue man
   alone before theAlone
   opening a door   as you dreamed

Gracias a EPoe, ARimbaud, FNietzsche, GWFHegel, WWhitman, JBaudrillard, PVirilio,
AKroker, DCook, JBierhorst, CCastaneda, Words of the Desert Fathers, & Chilam Balam